Catherine Cookson was born in Tyne Dock, the illegitimate daughter of a poverty-stricken woman, Kate, whom she believed to be her older sister. She began work in service but eventually moved south to Hastings where she met and married Tom Cookson, a local grammar-school master. At the age of forty she began writing about the lives of the working-class people with whom she had grown up, using the place of her birth as the background to many of her novels.

Although originally acclaimed as a regional writer – her novel *The Round Tower* won the Winifred Holtby award for the best regional novel of 1968 – her readership soon began to spread throughout the world. Her novels have been translated into more than a dozen languages and more than 50,000,000 copies of her books have been sold in Corgi alone. Many of her novels have been made into successful television dramas, and more are planned.

Catherine Cookson's many bestselling novels established her as one of the most popular of contemporary women novelists. After receiving an OBE in 1985, Catherine Cookson was created a Dame of the British Empire in 1993. She was appointed an Honorary Fellow of St Hilda's College, Oxford in 1997. For many years she lived near Newcastle-upon-Tyne. She died shortly before her ninety-second birthday in June 1998 having completed 104 works, nine of which are being published posthumously.

'Catherine Cookson's  hardship, the intractabili........................ruggle first to survive a...........................val. Humour, toughness..........................kson virtues, in a worl...........................and violent. Her novels........................her own early experiences.................poverty. This is what gives them power....... specialised world of women's popular fiction, Cookson has created her own territory'
Helen Dunmore, *The Times*

BOOKS BY CATHERINE COOKSON

NOVELS

Kate Hannigan
The Fifteen Streets
Colour Blind
Maggie Rowan
Rooney
The Menagerie
Slinky Jane
Fanny McBride
Fenwick Houses
Heritage of Folly
The Garment
The Fen Tiger
The Blind Miller
House of Men
Hannah Massey
The Long Corridor
The Unbaited Trap
Katie Mulholland
The Round Tower
The Nice Bloke
The Glass Virgin
The Invitation
The Dwelling Place
Feathers in the Fire
Pure as the Lily
The Mallen Streak
The Mallen Girl
The Mallen Litter
The Invisible Cord
The Gambling Man
The Tide of Life
The Slow Awakening

The Iron Façade
The Girl
The Cinder Path
Miss Martha Mary Crawford
The Man Who Cried
Tilly Trotter
Tilly Trotter Wed
Tilly Trotter Widowed
The Whip
Hamilton
The Black Velvet Gown
Goodbye Hamilton
A Dinner of Herbs
Harold
The Moth
Bill Bailey
The Parson's Daughter
Bill Bailey's Lot
The Cultured Handmaiden
Bill Bailey's Daughter
The Harrogate Secret
The Black Candle
The Wingless Bird
The Gillyvors
My Beloved Son
The Rag Nymph
The House of Women
The Maltese Angel
The Year of the Virgins
The Golden Straw
Justice is a Woman
The Tinker's Girl

A Ruthless Need | The Solace of Sin
The Obsession | Riley
The Upstart | The Blind Years
The Branded Man | The Thursday Friend
The Bonny Dawn | A House Divided
The Bondage of Love | Kate Hannigan's Girl
The Desert Crop | Rosie of the River
The Lady on My Left | The Silent Lady

THE MARY ANN STORIES

A Grand Man | Life and Mary Ann
The Lord and Mary Ann | Marriage and Mary Ann
The Devil and Mary Ann | Mary Ann's Angels
Love and Mary Ann | Mary Ann and Bill

FOR CHILDREN

Matty Doolin | Mrs Flannagan's Trumpet
Joe and the Gladiator | Go Tell It To Mrs Golightly
The Nipper | Lanky Jones
Rory's Fortune | Nancy Nutall and the Mongrel
Our John Willie | Bill and the Mary Ann
 | Shaughnessy

AUTOBIOGRAPHY

Our Kate | Let Me Make Myself Plain
Catherine Cookson Country | Plainer Still
None So Blind and other
    Poems

SHORT STORIES

The Simple Soul and other Stories

The Simple Soul

AND OTHER STORIES

CATHERINE COOKSON

CORGI BOOKS

THE SIMPLE SOUL AND OTHER STORIES
A CORGI BOOK : 0 552 14532 7

Originally published in Great Britain by Bantam Press,
a division of Transworld Publishers

PRINTING HISTORY
Bantam Press edition published 2001
Corgi edition published 2002

1 3 5 7 9 10 8 6 4 2

Set in 11/13pt Sabon by
Phoenix Typesetting, Ilkley, West Yorkshire.

Corgi Books are published by Transworld Publishers,
61–63 Uxbridge Road, London W5 5SA,
a division of The Random House Group Ltd,
in Australia by Random House Australia (Pty) Ltd,
20 Alfred Street, Milsons Point, Sydney, NSW 2061, Australia,
in New Zealand by Random House New Zealand Ltd,
18 Poland Road, Glenfield, Auckland 10, New Zealand
and in South Africa by Random House (Pty) Ltd,
Endulini, 5a Jubilee Road, Parktown 2193, South Africa.

Printed and bound in Germany by
Elsnerdruck, Berlin.

Contents

I

The Simple Soul

He looked at his wife's reflection in the bathroom mirror, and told himself it was impossible to hate her. But he did hate her; he hated her pale, cool face, her light brown hair, her figure that had never got any fatter in twelve years of married life. He had slept with this woman every night of those twelve years, and they hadn't been parted for a day . . . well, perhaps a day but never a night. He had loved her, laughed at her and with her, fought with her and against her, but never, until this moment, had he actually felt that he hated her.

The electric razor, making a quiet buzz against his cheekbone, began to shake.

'Would you mind switching that thing off for a moment?'

This was one of his reasons for hating her, this cool way she had of attacking him: would he mind switching that thing off for a moment! He switched it off so quickly that he stubbed his thumb.

Into the brittle silence her words came: 'I'm not asking you to consider the wife-end of this set-up, but it would be nice if you remembered that you have three children and but for "good morning" and "goodnight" they haven't seen you for a week. They would like it very much if you were to drive them down to the beach – that is, if you have nothing else in mind.'

The electric razor went spinning across the glass shelf, skidded over the edge and descended into the bath after completing a wall-of-death circuit.

He leant towards the mirror and watched his lips spitting out the words on to the cold surface: 'And what do you think the husband-end of the set-up has been doing all week? Two hours each morning in a blasted train to town, two hours in the evening coming back, and to what? To an aloof creature getting more like something out of a fashion magazine every night. Only the models don't wear that "How could you do this to me?" look.'

He swung round from the mirror and faced her. 'The trouble with you is that I play the game too clean,' he said. 'You've never had to wonder where I was, what I was up to. You've known my every move. Like a damn fool I've mapped it all out for you.'

He stopped, waiting for her to come back at him, her voice cool, her words incisive. But she remained silent, her skin looking paler, almost transparent. Then she did reply, but not in the way he expected. Her voice quiet, but with a slight tremor in it, she said, 'Richard, this has been going on for more than a year now, it's got to come to an end. We'll talk about it later.' Her head drooped just slightly, she turned towards the door; and then he had the bathroom to himself.

He bent over the bath and picked up what he was sure must be a damaged razor, and now he had the urge to throw it through the window and into the garden, perhaps to be returned by his sons Andy and Stephen who, in the miraculous way they seemed to have with the inside of clocks, might make it function once more and shave everything within sight.

He ran his hands through his hair, went back to the mirror and stared once again at his reflection. He didn't like what he saw. Lifting his hair up like that showed the two receding patches on his forehead; there were two deep grooves running from his nose downwards, past his mouth to the line of his jaw; and there was more than a suspicion of pouches under his eyes. He had never been handsome, but it was agreed that what he lacked in looks, had been compensated for in other ways: he had what was called a personality. Or he had had! Now there seemed to be nothing left but a temper that was burning him up. But could it be wondered at? Five long days a week slogging in town, and then at the weekends, jobs lined up for him before he got out of bed on a Saturday morning, which kept him going until he dropped thankfully into it again on a Sunday night. The alternative was: 'We must drop over to Mother's . . .' Mother lived a hundred and twenty miles away. 'We really must go and see Milly.' Milly lived only seventy miles away, but Milly had a bore of a husband and six undisciplined brats, who left him feeling as if he had just emerged from a rugger scrum. Another time it would be: 'We must get those bulbs in for Mother . . . Her bottom patch needs digging, her fence needs mending, her garage door is nearly off.'

The requests would have been preceded with a laughing, 'Come on, the chain gang!' and he would have approached the odd jobs perhaps with some irritation, but only simulated wrath. Not lately, however. And now this morning at breakfast she had implied that he was expected to take the lot of them to the beach, where, amid hordes of children, sun-boiled men and frowsty women oozing out of over-tight bathing costumes, he would have to spend the day and, what was more, enjoy it. Well, be damned if he was going to! He'd had enough. She wanted to talk, did she? Well, so did he, but in his own good time. He was sick of being pushed around, sick of it. He tore the comb through his hair, took his shirt off the back of the door, marched out of the bathroom across the landing and into the bedroom, the very sight of which irritated him. Yet some thought, forcing its way in through reason-ableness, proffered quietly: There was a time when you thought this the most wonderful room in the world and Annette the best home-maker, with a sense of colour second to none. She had a way with grey and lime, with mustard, sea-green and autumn brown that made a room different from any other, that made a bedroom different.

But one couldn't live with a combination of

colours; one wanted more than a house that was different.

Within three minutes Richard was running down the white staircase determinedly buttoning his coat.

Patricia was at the foot of the stairs. She was a tall eight and a replica of her mother. She looked at him with Annette's eyes now and said, 'You going out, Daddy?'

'Yes.' He was on his way to the front door.

'Where?'

'I don't know.'

She danced after him. 'Well, how will you get there, then?'

Wasn't that like her mother? He did not answer but hurried along the front of the house to the garage, where his eldest son was examining the car with a ten-year-old's critical eye. 'Back tyre wants some air, I think.'

'I wasn't asking you what you think. Get out of the way!'

'What's up with you?'

'Don't you dare speak to me in that way!' Father and son surveyed each other. 'It's about time you were taken in hand.'

He pulled open the car door, and the next minute the car was out of the garage.

Through the mirror he could see his boy, with head bent, looking at the ground. Some part of him was upset, but this only urged on Richard's departure.

He was out on the main road, where he

remained for the next forty miles. It was when a road sign said, 'You are now in Sussex', that he pulled on to the verge, and for the first time that day he relaxed against the seat – 'slumped' was more like it. He felt absolutely done in. Here, at half past eleven on a Saturday morning, he felt that he had just finished a heavy week . . . Well, hadn't he? He had had a very heavy week. That was what some people didn't understand. 'Some people' conjured up the face of Annette, and he swore under his breath.

Well, he was out on his own now, away from it all . . . and what was he going to do? He'd have lunch somewhere, have a good stiff drink, find a river and lie on the bank.

It was as he thought of a river that the name Jimmy rose to the surface of his mind, as if it had been washed there by the gentle lap of water. Jimmy. That was what he would do, he would go and see Jimmy. Jimmy lived in Sussex, didn't he? He looked around at the flowing fields as if they would answer him. Jimmy had been at him for years to pay him a visit.

Where was he? The last signpost had said, 'Hastings 28 miles'. Jimmy lived outside Battle in a cottage in a wood. At one time Jimmy had talked so much about that cottage that it was all he could do to restrain himself from shouting at his colleague, 'For heaven's sake, man, shut up!' Jimmy had been a bachelor when he bought the cottage, and Richard had always considered him a bit soft in the head for saddling himself with it. Three years later, when Jimmy got married, this seemed to prove it.

James Wheatley and he had started in the same office in Reynolds' Company when they were lads, and step by step they had moved up from the basement until they had to use the lift to the first floor. It wouldn't have done to have gone up the stairs, not when you were young and earnest and full of your own importance. Now he was on the fifth and only one from the top, whereas Jimmy was still on the first; but nearly every day he saw Jimmy, for his one-time colleague had the embarrassing habit of waiting for him and escorting him either to the bus or to the tube. He was the kind of man it was impossible to snub.

The cottage in the wood, the cottage Richard felt he knew, took quite a time to find. Several times he stopped the car then traversed a number of side roads before he came to the farm. He felt he knew the farm too. The farmer's wife said, 'Oh, the Wheatleys. Oh, yes. But you can't get the car down to them. Leave it over there' – she pointed – 'so the cattle won't get round it, and then go through that gate and across the fields and you'll be at the cottage in no time.'

It was about fifteen minutes later when Richard saw it. He was on a rise and stood looking down on it in amazement. It was whitewashed, or had been, tiny and, from this distance, it seemed almost buried in a tangle of undergrowth. But when he approached the front door he saw that there had been some attempt to make a garden. And he should know this garden. With nerve-tearing irritation, he had listened to all Jimmy was doing in it, propagating rhododendrons, enlarging his azalea stocks through cuttings . . . he had marvellous azaleas!

The door was half open, and now wishing that he had never thought of Jimmy and his cottage, he leant forward and tapped twice.

He just stopped himself letting his mouth drop into a wide gape when he saw the woman. He did not doubt that she was Jimmy's wife: Jimmy had described her to him time and time again. He knew all her virtues, but most of all he knew what she looked like: she was a ravishing blonde or as near it as made no odds. 'Her hair isn't gold,' Jimmy had said, 'it's silver, and she hasn't blue eyes like an ordinary blonde, they're grey.' The combination had sounded decidedly attractive, yet he had wondered at the time why any blonde, unless she was really dim, should throw in her lot with Jimmy . . . and now he knew.

The woman's hair might have been silver many, many years ago but now it was a tacky dull mess. The eyes were still grey but whatever allure they had once had was now dimmed by a network of lines round them, as were her upper lips. Years ago, the woman's face and figure might have caused an eyebrow to rise, but now they would evoke only pity, if anything.

The woman stared at him. She did not smile but her eyes widened slightly then narrowed. 'You're Dicky Morton, aren't you?'

'Yes. Yes, I am, and' – he made himself smile – 'you're Mrs Wheatley?'

'Yes, I am.' It sounded defensive. 'Come in. I'll tell Jimmy. He's out in the field at the back.'

He followed her into what was presumably the main room of the cottage. Disorder was not the word he would have used to describe it, but a phrase his mother had been apt to throw at him about the condition of his bedroom came back to him: 'utter clutter'. Here, indeed, was utter clutter. The woman, however, made no apology for it. She pointed to a chair and said, 'Sit down, and I'll call him.'

He watched her move out of the room. She seemed in no hurry. But then he got a further surprise when he heard her call, 'Oo-oo! Darling!'

Oo-oo, darling, he repeated to himself, and shook his head, mystified. Almost within the next minute Jimmy was in the room, Jimmy in his shirt-sleeves and old trousers with a grin on his face that embarrassed Richard with the sincerity of its welcome.

'Why, Dicky, if this isn't a surprise! You've got round to it at last.' He was pumping Richard's hand up and down and, still holding it, he turned to his wife where she stood leaning against the table and explained, 'Didn't I tell you? I told you he'd pop in one of these days.' Turning back to Richard, he said, 'I've no need to tell you who she is, have I?' Then straightening, his hands hanging limply at his sides now, the smile slid off his face to leave it with a look of contentment. His voice now matching his expression, he said softly, 'By, Dicky, I'm glad to see you. Oh, I am.'

It was as if they hadn't met for twenty years but it had been scarcely twenty hours since they had parted.

'Have you the wife with you, and the children?'

'No, no. I just came out for a run and found myself in Sussex and I thought, well . . . well, I'd look you up.'

'Well, well, what a pity! We'd have made a day of it.' Reaching out, he pulled his wife towards him, his arm encircling her waist as he went on, 'What have we got left?' Then he blushed and grinned again boyishly. 'There I go, talking as if I didn't know! We've got half a bottle of sherry – it's been there since my birthday. Anyway we'll finish it – what do you say, Flo?'

Flo. And, metaphorically speaking, Richard closed his eyes. He knew her name was Florence, but Flo, a worn-out blonde, blowsy. In the name of heaven! Where had Jimmy picked her up? And yet it was more than likely that she had picked him up. Yes, she looked the type. Suddenly he felt a deep compassion for Jimmy, for being so gullible.

Jimmy had disappeared through the door, and while Richard looked at the woman, and she looked at him, he could still hear Jimmy talking, still exclaiming about the wonder of his visit. The amazing thing was that Jimmy was genuinely pleased to see him, not a bit ashamed of this woman or this house . . . the dream cottage in a wood. How deeply could one delude oneself? If anyone was suffering under a delusion then Jimmy was.

The woman startled him into stiffness when she said, 'Don't look so surprised.'

'What?'

'I said, don't look so surprised.'

He smiled slightly as if he didn't know what she was referring to. 'What do you mean?'

'You know what I mean,' and she turned towards her husband as he entered the room, saying, 'I'll see to the lunch.'

'You'll do no such thing – well, not for a tick. You'll have a drink first.' Here was a masterful Jimmy.

'But the chicken's on. It'll be burnt. I'll be back in a minute.'

'All right, darling, just as you say.' The voice was meek again; the real Jimmy. And now he turned to Richard and said, 'We must have known you were coming, we're having a chicken for lunch. Flo's a marvellous cook. Just you wait, you're in for a treat. Well, here's to you.' He handed Richard a glass of sherry and bent forward, almost hovering over him in his pleasure. It was most embarrassing . . . the whole set-up. But it had taken his mind off Annette, at least for the present.

The lunch had been well cooked, but it was ordinary, nothing startling: roast chicken, sage and onion stuffing, roast potatoes and sprouts, a rice pudding afterwards, of all things, and to cap it . . . a cup of tea.

Richard would have liked to escape immediately

after lunch but Jimmy made it awkward for him. First, he would have to see round the cottage – this didn't take long – then the garden. Undoubtedly Jimmy had not lied when he talked of his rhododendrons and azaleas, but the majority of them were nearly choked with bramble. Jimmy explained that it was difficult to get the gardening done in a weekend, and Flo was no hand at it. Besides, she wasn't strong at all. This last was stated in a solemn tone. It was the only point of the whole meeting when some sort of a smile had not been on Jimmy's face. And then his wife had called from the house . . . They hadn't any milk!

Jimmy explained that he collected it each evening on his return but on a Saturday and Sunday he went up for it in the afternoon. 'I won't ask you to come along,' he said. 'You'd tear your suit to shreds. I take a short-cut through the hedges. Anyway,' and here he nudged Richard, 'I want you and Flo to get acquainted, have a natter on your own.' He jerked his head proudly as if he were presenting Richard with an opportunity that should not be missed.

Richard had no desire to crawl through hedges and tear his suit, but he had less desire to sit with Flo; but that was exactly what he was doing, and he knew that in a way this was what she wanted. He watched her light a cigarette, then lean back against the padded couch and blow out the smoke with what he termed cheap expertise before she startled him once again. 'If you try to open Jimmy's eyes in any way I'll pay you back . . . I might even go so far as to kill you.'

He was sitting bolt upright in his chair. 'I don't understand, what do you mean?'

'Come off it.' She sounded as common as she looked. If she had been taking the part of a worn-out street-walker in a play he would have thought her well cast. 'Jimmy thinks I'm nice. Jimmy thinks I'm the goods, and I am the goods. As long as I have him I'll be the goods.'

'What has this to do with me?' His voice had a cold ring to it.

'Everything. You see, I know all about you, and I think I've hated you from the first week I knew Jimmy. You were too blooming good to be true. He's a child, is Jimmy: he's still playing with fairies at the bottom of the garden. I think he's the only one left in this rotten world who still believes in people. You've climbed up the firm and Jimmy's been happy for you, even though he's been left behind. To Jimmy you're a big brain, handsome, athletic. You're everything in *Boys' Own Weekly*. He's as blind about you as he is about me, because you're not a big brain, and you're not handsome or athletic; you've got bags under your eyes and you've got the beginnings of a paunch. And you've got a rotten temper. Also I'm not wrong in thinking that you came here today not to see him or even to find out what I was like but just to pass the time . . . Right?'

'You're being insulting.'

'Well, that fits in with your picture of me, doesn't it? I mean, the real picture, not the one that Jimmy has given you. You know . . .' she leant forward, her forearms on her knees, her hands drooping between them, there was something masculine in the action, something threatening '. . . I'm fighting to hold on to something, something that you can kill. You see Jimmy every day. Even a child's eyes can be opened to the truth if it's rammed in hard and subtly enough. So don't do it. I'm warning you, don't do it.'

He stared at the woman. All this was fantastic, yet it was true. Every word she had said was true.

He heard himself saying, 'You needn't worry. Why should I open Jimmy's eyes? And can you be sure that they need to be opened? Perhaps he's just playing a game of his own.'

'Jimmy's playing no game, he's an innocent. I've been married three times before and I should know.'

Richard's chin moved down and his eyes with it. He wasn't at all surprised.

He jerked upright as she said, 'You're not at all surprised, are you?'

Meeting her on her own ground now, he said, 'I wouldn't have taken you for an innocent teenager.'

She stared at him, and to his amazement, her lips began to tremble and she bit the lower one in an attempt to steady it. She turned and stubbed out the cigarette. Her voice was different now as she said, 'I don't suppose I could convince you that I ever was.' She looked away from him as she went on, 'I was married when I was sixteen. He was a stoker and went to sea. Before I was nineteen I had lost two babies, stillborn. He was drowned when I was twenty. I can only remember how relieved I was. When I was twenty-four I married again. This one was lazy. I worked for him for four years until he had to join up. He was torpedoed in 1941. In 1945 I married a refined man – so refined that he could have charmed the Queen to put a signature to a cheque. You mightn't believe it but I wanted refinement, I craved it in a way. Out of the ten years I was married to him he was a guest of Her Majesty's Prison Service for eight of them. We didn't see much of each other and I had to work again. I always had to work . . .' and now her eyes were again on Richard '. . . until I met Jimmy. Jimmy is what you would call soft in the head, so he fell for me.'

Richard looked away from her. It was uncanny how this woman read his mind. He kept his eyes lowered as she went on, 'All Jimmy wanted was to work for me, to love me, to protect me . . . He thinks I need protection. I've been married to Jimmy for four years and when he brought me to this neck of the woods I wondered how to God I was going to stand it, although I liked Jimmy then. Now I love him, and I want nothing more on this earth than to remain here with him. You wouldn't be able to understand that.'

'Why shouldn't I?'

They remained looking at each other, in silence now, and it was strange but he found that he *did* understand this woman. He didn't think he could say he liked her or that he understood why Jimmy loved her so wholeheartedly, but he did understand her desire to be loved, protected. He understood it because he had lived for twelve years with Annette. He had felt like that about Annette when they were first married. Oh . . . oh, and long after. He had wanted to be loved, fussed over and, if not actually protected, made secure by love, and Annette had done that. Annette had been warm and loving and giving, but what had he given in return? All his life he had wanted to be fussed over, listened to. Annette had always been there to listen to him when he returned from the office, and he couldn't get back quickly enough to his audience. That was what Annette had been to him: a loving audience.

He rose to his feet. He hated the idea that he had been forced to see himself through this woman's eyes. But now that he had he could no longer shut his ears to the voice that said, 'It's taken you a long time to grow up.' He was in his forties and it wasn't nice to discover that he had only just grown up; he needed no bathroom mirror to see himself. The trouble between Annette and him had started over a year ago when she had become tired of listening, and when – because of the heavy work entailed in his swift rise up those office floors – he had become tired in his loving.

All of a sudden he was overwhelmed by terror and through it he could hear Annette's flat, unemotional voice saying, 'We will have to talk.'

The woman, too, was on her feet, an arm's length from him now, and her face was twitching as she spoke. 'What's the matter? You're not going straight away? He'd wonder . . . And you needn't look like that. There's nothing I've done that I'm

24

ashamed of, not really. It's only looking like I do. I know how I look.'

He was staring at her. Then, without thinking, he put one hand out to her, then the other, and then he was clasping hers tightly and talking quickly: 'Don't worry, please! It isn't that . . . Well, you see, you've brought me to my senses in a way. Yes, yes, I was surprised about you. No good trying to hood-wink you, because I showed it, but—'

'But you still pity Jimmy?'

'No. No, I don't. Why should I?'

She pulled her hands quickly away from his. 'Ssh! Here he is. You'll not go yet?'

As he said, 'No, no, of course not,' he wanted to get into the car and go home, home to Annette, but he stayed. And he behaved as if he was happy to stay . . .

It was nearly five o'clock when they walked with him across the fields up to the farm. Before he got into his car Jimmy placed his hand on Richard's shoulder and said solemnly, 'This has been the happiest day of my life, Richard.' Casting a glance at Flo, he added, with a smile, 'Well, almost, bar our wedding day, but Flo understands.'

Richard looked at Flo. She looked happier, more at ease, but she didn't look any younger, any better. To him she still looked a drab, worn-out blonde. Yet taking her hand once more he asked humbly, 'May I bring my wife along some day to see you?'

There was a pause before she answered quietly, 'She'll be welcome.'

'Welcome! I should say she'd be welcome.' Jimmy

slapped him on the shoulder as he got into the car; and then, with one arm around Flo's shoulders, he stood waving until his friend disappeared.

Once away there was one thought in Richard's head: he must look out for a call-box. At last he found one.

As he lifted the receiver his hands trembled. A few minutes later, not being able to get through, he left. Perhaps she was in the garden, but even there she would have heard it ring. Well, very likely she had taken a walk with the children.

He was in a deserted side road when the car stopped. Looking at the dial, he couldn't believe he was out of petrol, but he was. It took him a quarter of an hour to find a garage and get a can of petrol back to the car. At the garage, he had asked if he could use the phone. Again, there had been no reply.

He couldn't really believe his ill luck when, only forty miles from home, he had a puncture. Now it was almost dark. By the time he had changed the wheel he was panicking: everything seemed to be conspiring against him, keeping him away from his home and Annette. Before he started the car again he felt compelled to phone once more. He was in a village and the call-box was only a few yards from him. When, for the third time, there was no reply he leant against it. It was nine o'clock. The children should have been in bed this past hour. Annette was very strict about bedtime. Anyway, if they were in, Andy was capable of answering the phone. But if the children were in Annette would be in: she never left them alone. Frantically now, he searched through the directory for the Beales' number. The Beales were their neighbours in the next detached house. They were at present away on holiday but their friend Miss Carter was looking after the place and the dogs. She would be in.

Miss Carter said, 'Hello, who's that?'

He said, 'It's Richard Morton. I've had trouble with my car, Miss Carter, I wonder if you would tell my wife I've not been able to get through. There must be something wrong with the line.'

'Oh, Mr Morton, there's no-one in. Well, there's no lights on and I saw them all going away this afternoon. Didn't you know?'

His voice sounded rusty as he repeated, 'Away!' then asked, 'Where?'

'Well, I don't know, Mr Morton, but Mrs Morton was carrying a suitcase.'

After a pause he made himself laugh, and he answered loudly, 'Yes. Yes, of course, they were going to her mother's. Thank you, Miss Carter. Goodbye.'

When he got into the car he sat quite still for some minutes before he lit a cigarette. He remained sitting there quietly until he had finished it. Then, still slowly, as if he were very tired, he started the car and drove home.

As Miss Carter had said, there were no lights on. He let himself in, walked through the hall, into the drawing room and switched on the central lights. Everything was as he knew it yet different, more beautiful, because it was no longer home. He had lost it. He sat down and lit another cigarette. He just couldn't believe it had happened. What did a man do in a case like this? Get drunk and say, 'To hell'? He couldn't do that, he could just moan inwardly, Oh, Annette. Oh, Annette.

His elbows were on his knees and his hands were supporting his face when the voice came at him. His surprise was so great that his elbows slipped from his knees and he fell forward. Annette was standing in the doorway in her dressing-gown. Her face was whiter than he had ever seen it, her eyes larger, and there was a sadness about her that tore at him. She said, 'Do you want anything to eat?'

'The car ran out of petrol, then I got a puncture. I tried to get you three times.'

She moved slowly towards the fireplace. 'The Arnolds phoned,' she said. 'The boys wanted the children to go out to the farm. They asked if they could stay overnight. I took them this afternoon. I haven't been back long.'

'Annette. Annette . . . Oh, Annette.' He rushed to her and almost carried her to the couch. Her arms went about him, and he was actually crying.

She said, 'There, there! What is it? Oh, Richard, what is it?'

Shamefacedly, he wiped his face. Then lifting his head from her shoulder, he said, 'I love you, Annette.'

'Oh, darling!' She was shaking with relief. And now she, too, was crying. 'I was so worried. You didn't say where you were going. Oh, I've been so worried . . . Where did you go?'

'To Jimmy's . . . you know Jimmy?'

'But – but why to him? I – I thought you didn't get on. I thought he was . . . well, sort of a simple soul.'

'He is, but he's the happiest man I know. I think I went to him because I knew he was happy, and he is, absolutely . . . You see it was like this.'

He went on talking, talking, talking, and she went on listening and stroking and patting. 'Things will be different now . . . *I*'ll be different.' She smiled quietly into the crook of his arm. He had promised so many things, among them not to impose on her capacity as an audience. It was funny when she thought about it, for he had been talking steadily for an hour now. But what did that matter? Their world was right once more, things were back to where they had been before the pattern of their marriage had altered. It was right for them that he should talk and she should listen. That pattern was right for them, as the pattern was right, apparently, for that simple soul and his Flo.

2

The Forbidden Word

1924

At the far end of the long yard, the light streaming from the kitchen window showed a bent figure about to pick up a bucket of coal.

Sally Smythe watched her sister's head turn slowly towards her, then her body snap upright; she watched her take three steps forward, the coat she had over her head slip on to her shoulders, and the lightly falling snow settle on her dark hair. The whisper came to her now, sounding colder than the night: 'Eeh, our Sally. My God! No!'

They both remained still, peering at each other until the elder girl's hand jerked out and, gripping her sister's shoulder, she dragged her towards the wash-house door. Pushing it open, she pulled her inside. Then in the dim light, as if she had been running, she stood gasping before she muttered, 'Eeh, God! There'll be murder done.'

What penetrated the young girl's mind at this moment was her sister's use of God's name twice within the last few seconds. In a way it foretold what was to come.

'He'll kill you. You must be mad to come back here like that.' She almost whimpered as she said, 'And Harry's people, they wouldn't stand for this.' Then her voice rose as she cried, 'Oh, you! You would do something like this, wouldn't you? Well, I wouldn't like to be in your shoes at this minute, I wouldn't that.'

'Where is he?' The girl's tone gave no indication of her feelings.

'In the front room. There's a committee meeting. The Reverend's there and the warden.'

'Where's Ma?'

'In the kitchen. She's bakin'. It's our Harry's Susie's birthday the morrow. But you wouldn't remember that, would you? No, no . . . Oh, Lord above!'

'I'm sorry, Betty. I am.'

'Sorry, you say? Sorry? If you were sorry you wouldn't have landed with a bellyful like that.'

'Well, I have landed, so I'd better get it over, hadn't I?' Her voice was small: the fear that had kept her away until this last moment was running rampant again.

'Get it over, you say? You'll be lucky if you get out alive. You must be mad – stark staring mad. You know what he's like. He watches us, Ted an' me, and we've got the date fixed, but we can't have a minute alone. Oh!'

She flounced out of the wash-house, grabbed the

bucket of coal, then stumbled up the yard. Sally followed her, but slowly, very slowly.

Her mother was standing at the kitchen table. She had just finished rolling out pastry, presumably for tarts, for as she put the rolling-pin down, she picked up a crinkled-edged cutter. But it never reached the pastry: she held it hovering in the air above the floured board while her eyes swept over the figure of her snow-covered daughter, then came to rest where the middle button of the blue serge coat exposed a wide red V-shape both above and below itself. She gaped, and dropped the cutter, then seemed to stagger. She turned her eyes on her elder daughter, and said, ''Tisn't true, is it, Betty? I'm – I'm seeing things. Tell me 'tisn't true.'

'It's true right enough, Ma.'

'Oooh! Girl, what have you done? I – I can't believe it. Oh, dear God!'

At the sound of raised voices from the other room she suddenly put her hand tight over her mouth, at the same time turning an agonised look towards the door and crying quietly as if in prayer, 'Oh, Lord! Lord!'

At this, Betty said, 'She shouldn't stay, Ma. He'll do something – go mad, clean mad.'

'Yes, you're right. You're right, Betty.'

They both looked at Sally now, and she swallowed before she said, 'Where would I go, Ma? I've nowhere else.'

'You should have thought of that before . . .' her mother seemed to search for words then finished in a rush '. . . before you let yourself go loose.'

'I didn't go loose. I thought I was going to be married.'

'Then why aren't you?'

Before she could answer there came the sound of a commotion in the passage and a series of voices saying, 'Goodnight', followed by the closing of the front door.

Sally watched her mother and sister move quickly away from the table and take up positions close together beside a chest of drawers in the corner of the room. The door leading from the passage was to the right of them and both were looking towards it. It opened, then closed, and there stood her father.

Robert Smythe was a man of medium height; he was of bony thinness, with grey hair, and his eyebrows too were turning grey. He had round dark eyes, a high-bridged nose and a shapeless mouth, but, unlike his wife's, it did not fall open when he recognised his daughter's condition. After a full minute of staring at her he turned to where his wife and elder daughter were standing and asked, in a deep, bass voice, 'Who is this?'

His wife gulped audibly, then said, 'She has nowhere else to go.'

'No?' It was a question.

Now he slowly advanced towards the table and nodded at Sally. Then he gripped the edge, leant across and cried, 'How dare you? How dare you come into this house in that condition? You filthy little slut, you! And after the way you've been brought up, in a God-fearing family . . . You! You!'

His thin lips moved convulsively as if he were trying to swallow something, and there was a rumble in his throat before he hissed, 'Horsewhipping! That's what you want – horsewhipping. You should be stripped to the pelt and horsewhipped. You lying daughter of the devil, you. You couldn't come home in the summer because you said you were going on holiday with the family you were working for, and we believed you. You went on holiday all right, didn't you? *Didn't you?*'

As his hand flashed out and grabbed the rolling-pin, Jennie Smythe sprang forward and caught her husband's arm, crying, 'No, no! She'll go! She'll go, Robert. It can be dealt with quietly. Nobody need ever know.' As if she were explaining to a child, she pointed to the window, crying, 'It's dark. No-one saw her come. Nobody saw you come, did they?' she appealed to her daughter.

Sally made no response. Strangely, the fear she had lived with for weeks, knowing that she would have to make this journey, knowing that she would have to confront her tyrant of a father, had suddenly disappeared. She saw him for what he was, what she had always known him to be: a sanctimonious, frustrated hypocrite.

Of course, no word could be said against him for visiting people because he was a collector for the drapery store – but she knew it didn't take three hours in one cottage to collect a weekly payment. She had been passing on her bike when she saw him go in, and hours later, when she was coming back that way, she had seen him come out.

Now her mother was gabbling: 'She needn't stay here. Nobody need know. I'll give her the money to go back to Harrogate. She can have it there. I've got some saved. Look – look, I'll go and get it.' She was still holding on to his arm as she turned now to Betty, crying, 'Stay with him until I get it. Stay with him!'

As her mother rushed from the room, Betty went to take the rolling-pin from her father's hand, but he thrust her aside. His face suffused with fury, he growled at his younger daughter, 'She's not giving you any money. Make your way back as you made your way here. Work on the streets, you filthy, godless hussy, you.'

Her case had been on the floor by her side and now, slowly, Sally stooped and picked it up. Then, looking straight at him, she said, 'You're one to talk. Remember Mrs Hilda Pratt? I wonder, if the Church knew about her, what they would say to their highly respected churchwarden?'

She screamed and jumped at the same time as the rolling-pin whizzed past her head and crashed into a small mirror hanging on the wall, shattering it. Clutching her case, she ran to the door and out into the night.

In the back lane, she leant against the wall, and, tears raining down her cheeks, she asked herself where she could go, where she could find shelter. She wouldn't dare go to any of the neighbours, for that would finish him, and likely her too. There was her brother, Harry, but Harry's wife hated the sight of her – always had, because Harry had been so fond of her. No, she couldn't go to Harry's, so there was only one other place.

'You've left it a bit late, haven't you?' The infirmary porter stared down at her, then added as an afterthought, 'Both ways. You look froze. Sit over by the fire there. The portress is off duty but the labour mistress will be down in a minute.'

Five minutes later the labour mistress repeated the porter's words: 'You've left it a bit late, haven't you? When is it due?'

'Any time.'

'Where have you come from?'

'Harrogate.'

'Why didn't you stay there and have it?' The square face under the frilled white cap was expressionless.

It was some seconds before Sally answered: 'I had a friend here, but . . . but she's moved.'

'Where are your people?'

Again, seconds passed. 'I . . . I haven't any.'

'What was your last address in Harrogate?' She gave the woman the address of her lodgings.

'You know you'll be for the workhouse until it's born, and then after?'

She hadn't known, so she didn't answer.

'Have you any lice in your hair?'

'*No.*'

'Don't you shout at me, miss. Get along there to the bathroom and get your clothes off. You'll stay here in the casual ward until tomorrow morning and we'll see what's to be done with you then.'

*   *   *

Three days later her child was born. It was a girl, healthy and lusty. The following week Sally was sent down from the infirmary to the workhouse. At night she slept in the upper nursery, the child in a cot by her side. There were three other mothers with her, but as the days passed and they found she wasn't to be drawn, they talked among themselves and at her: people who were too big for their boots shouldn't be in there, should they?

If you didn't have visitors when you had a bairn there wasn't much hope of them coming later.

If there was no-one to take your bairn, what was your future? Fourteen years' hard labour until the bairn could be sent out to fend for itself, by which time you'd be as barmy as the majority of them in the workhouse. In fact, it was known that some folks couldn't stand it and they were sent up next door into Barnes's Wing, and the staff there were strait-jacket experts.

At night she lay awake, mulling over the talk, and she came to the conclusion that, yes, they were right, she would likely go mad if she had to stick this out for fourteen years, because half the inmates were unhinged.

For the first three months she was given light work, attending to the babies in the day nursery downstairs. Then, for no apparent reason that she could think of, except that the labour mistress didn't like her because she had shouted at her on their first meeting, she was put on the corridors.

They were stone-flagged and long, and had to be scrubbed daily. During the first week she cried every night because of the pain in her knees. When the nursery nurse saw them, Sally was immediately taken off the corridors and put on to Number One ward.

Even the other inmates held their noses when passing Number One ward. Here, in one long room, lay the diseased and the dying. Attached to it was a day room where those with arthritis and other disabling conditions sat. Some were comparatively young women, doomed for the remainder of their lives to inhale the smell of urine and decay.

After a few days of handling filthy sheets, Sally thought that she would rather be back on the corridors. Then, slowly, life changed; it even took on a cheerful aspect.

There were two women in wheelchairs who sat side by side in the day room: one was Mrs Ryan, and the other Mrs Ridley. Mrs Ryan was well into her seventies; Mrs Ridley, whose husband had deserted her when he learned her arthritis was incurable, was nearing forty. They both had a keen sense of humour, which, as Mrs Ryan explained to Sally, was a great pity as this was what had stopped her dying fifteen years ago when she had first come into the workhouse.

Both women were badly crippled and must have been in pain most of the time, yet they always smiled at her and joked in an endeavour to make her laugh. As time went on their kindness drew her out of herself.

Strangely, their plight gave her hope. She wouldn't go mad, she told herself, she would stick it out. Even so, it was daunting to think that she would be quite old when her daughter was fourteen. What life would there be for her when she was thirty-two?

Mrs Ryan always had someone to see her on visiting days, generally her nephew, whom she called Fred. Mrs Ridley, like Sally, had no-one, so on a Saturday afternoon Sally sat with her. Even when the sun was shining and she could have walked in the parade yard, she still sat with Mrs Ridley. And as time went on, Fred included her in the conversation . . . He had always included Mrs Ridley.

Sally had been in the workhouse for close on a year and she had never laughed aloud until she laughed at Fred McCall. And Mrs Ryan and Mrs Ridley had both exclaimed, 'There, now. There, now,' as if they had achieved something.

On that particular Saturday he was talking about his father. Sitting opposite the two wheelchairs, he looked from one to the other, then let his gaze rest on Sally for a moment before asking tentatively, 'Are you a Catholic?'

She shook her head, then said quietly, 'No.'

'Well, then, I'd say you're lucky. You haven't got to worry about lodgings in the hereafter.' He was nodding at his aunt as he went on, 'You know, me da feels sure they'll have a semi-detached up above for him the minute he kicks the bucket. But me ma's more for a bungalow, because of her legs, you know.' At this Mrs Ryan and Mrs Ridley laughed uproariously.

When Mrs Ryan asked now after his sister Maggie's children, Fred raised his hands as if in blessing and closed his eyes. 'Oh, Aunt Mary, you wouldn't believe it, but since little Marie has been picked for the Virgin Mary in the Nativity play, it's canonisation for Willy. Well, it couldn't be anything else, Aunt Mary, now could it?, since he begot her.'

They were all laughing, tears running down the older women's faces. Sally's head was turned away and her body was shaking: it wasn't so much what this fellow Fred said as the way he said it. Then a strange thing happened: suddenly she was plunged into the same depth of sadness that filled her nights. It became instantly unbearable. Rising to her feet, her head bowed, she left the ward hurriedly and went into the corridor. There, she stood looking out of the long windows on to the yard where some inmates were sitting on benches and others were peering through the iron railings that bordered the road outside.

'What is it? Was it something I said? I – I act the goat a bit, I know. It's – it's just to cheer them up. I'm sorry.' He was standing by her side now.

She turned her tear-stained face towards him, saying, 'It wasn't you, of course not. It was just . . . well, things.' She looked out of the window again.

'You haven't any people at all?'

She didn't answer.

'You know something? It's very strange, I must tell you this. You . . . you put me in mind of somebody I knew years ago – well, three or four years ago. You're the spit of her in a way, you know. She was a young lass who used to work in the paper shop in Frederick Street. She was very bonny. I only saw her a few times because I was moved across the water to a new job. I'm a riveter in the docks, you know, an' when I came back she was gone. They always say everybody has a double.' He didn't speak for some minutes, and then he said, 'How's your baby?'

'She's . . . she's fine, very well, growing.'

He was looking out of the window, too, as he said, 'How do you stand it in here?'

She swung round to him and, her lips trembling, she ground out through her teeth, 'I stand it because I've got to.' She went to move away, but he caught her arm, saying, 'I'm sorry. I . . . I seem to be saying all the wrong things for you today, but . . . but I'm just sorry that . . . well, that a young lass like you is stuck in here. Are you sure you have no people?'

She blinked, gulped, then said quietly, 'Not any who want to know.'

'Eeh, dear God! Don't tell me you really have somebody belonging to you and they don't know?'

'Oh, they know. Oh, yes, they know.'

'God almighty! Are they in Harrogate?'

She shook her head.

Now he said, in a whisper, 'Don't tell me they live here in Shields?' When she remained silent, he muttered, 'The things people do.' Then, with his face screwed up, he added, 'You mean to say they know you're in here . . . ?'

'No, they don't know I'm in here. They couldn't stand that, particularly him.' Her voice faded.

'But . . . wouldn't they come round if they knew the way you're placed?'

She turned to face him: 'My father's a member of the Church. They're all Church.'

'Methodists?'

'No, ordinary.' She smiled quizzically.

'Eeh! I thought our lot was bad, what with prejudice and this and that. But I can't see them lettin' one of their own come in here unless it was through dire poverty.'

She jerked her chin upwards as she said, 'Huh! There's five mothers now in the nursery and three of them are Catholics.'

He let out a deep laugh and exclaimed, 'You don't say.'

'I do.'

They smiled at each other. Then he said, 'Well, you could say they're all tarred with the same brush.'

A bell clanged and he turned to look down the corridor towards the ward door. 'Time, gentlemen, please. I'd better go and say goodbye to them.' Then he turned back to her and added quietly, 'Is there anything you would like me to bring in for you?'

'No, thank you.'

'There must be something.'

'I – I don't want anything.'

'Oh, well, we'll see. Until next week, then.'

She made no reply but turned to the window again as he went back to the ward.

*　　*　　*

The next Saturday he was accompanied by his sister Maggie, who looked at Sally and said, 'Don't I know you?'

Sally remained silent, staring wide-eyed at the plump woman.

'You used to serve in the paper shop in Frederick Street, didn't you?'

'I never did.'

'I could have sworn I'd seen you before.'

'You're mistaken.'

The following week they stood by the window again. The recreation yard was covered with snow, but there were still a few inmates outside. They were the ones who stood every Saturday near the iron railings, gazing out on to the road.

Fred kept his eyes directed towards the yard as he said, 'You did work in the paper shop, didn't you, Sally? And your family live in Pickerton Street.'

She swung round, muttering, 'You've been busy, haven't you? Why can't you mind your own business?'

'Well, because' – he pursed his lips – 'funny like, but you've become me business, sort of. Your da's known to be a ranter, isn't he? Mad Church. They're worse than us lot when they get going, the Protestants. Do you like me?'

She had turned to the window again, and the steam from her breath as she let it out in a slow hiss obliterated the view for a moment. Then she shook

44

her head, but did not speak. He said again, 'I asked you a question. Do you like me?'

Now she was looking at him, her words coming from between her teeth as she said, 'What a question to ask me, and me in this place!'

'It's got nothin' to do with you bein' in here. Well, I want an answer.'

She hung her head as she said, 'You're all right.'

'Is that all? I don't just think you're all right, because I've cottoned on to you, hard and fast. I can't get you out of me mind. Would you marry me?'

Now she started and, her voice soft and her eyes wide, she said, 'You'd marry me with the bairn?'

'Well, I won't marry you without her.'

'Oh, Fred!'

'That's the first time you've called me by me name. You would then, would you?'

When her head drooped, he moved closer to her, saying, 'Aw, don't start to cry. Don't, else one of those brass-faced attendants will come along. But that one on the ward, Aunt Mary's, she seems all right, she speaks well of you. I'll tell you something.' He now caught hold of her hand and pressed it between his own two rough ones. 'I'm going to see about takin' you out for a day.'

'Oh, no, no, they'll not allow that.'

'You never know what they'll allow. I happen to know the assistant master. He carries some weight. He was my Scoutmaster when I was a kid and we've been friendly ever since.' He laughed now as he added, 'I wasn't in the Scouts long. Me da hoicked me out when he realised I was spouting Protestant prayers. Anyway, I'm going to see about taking you out on Saturday soon.'

'Oh!' She smiled at him, then said, 'But what if I do a bunk?'

'Oh, that's what he said, Mr Moreton.'

'You've seen him about it already?'

'Well, aye, I have. I don't let the grass grow under me feet, not when I want anything as badly as I want you.' His voice had dropped to a low note, and now he finished, 'You know what'll happen if you do a bunk? I'll be responsible for the bairn, I'll have to pay for her keep. So don't you do any bunks.'

For a brief moment their brows touched and their soft laughter mingled.

Patrick McCall looked at his sister and, his voice thick, he said, 'Chrissy's nearly up the pole, our David taking his vows in three months' time and our Fred coming home sayin' he's gonna marry a piece who's in here, and her with a bairn. And if that isn't enough, she's a Protestant, from a ranter's family.'

Mary Ryan shook her head, 'Look, our Patrick, the girl's a good girl—'

'Good girl!' Patrick interrupted. 'How did she come in? Good girl, you say? Her on nineteen and got a bairn! She started early.'

'No earlier than your own Maggie.' Mary Ryan's voice was low. 'I don't know how you had the nerve to send her up the aisle in white. And it didn't hood-wink Father Bradley into thinking he only had two kneeling afore him at the altar rails. There was two and a good half there for she was nearly five months gone. So you, our Patrick, don't forget who you're talkin' to. And I repeat, she's a good girl, and Fred's fallen for her and he'll have her.'

'By God, he won't, not if I can help it. I'll have Father O'Keefe along at the house the night. He'll talk sense into him.'

'Do that. I'd like to be there.' A grin spread over her face as she ended, 'I wouldn't be surprised at the end of the conversation if poor Father O'Keefe will have decided to give up the cloth.'

Patrick stood up and, looking down on his sister, he said, 'I can see no help from this quarter. It's hard to believe that you're me own sister, brought up in the faith, yet you'd welcome a ranter and her bairn. All I can say is, God forgive you. Yes, God forgive you.' Then he turned on his heel and marched from the room.

Mrs Ridley, leaning towards Mary, said, 'What if he puts his spoke in?'

Mary's answer was brief. 'My money's on Fred.'

It was a month later. It had been a bright sunny Saturday and Sally had been out since ten o'clock in the morning and now she and Fred were standing outside in the shelter of the wall to the side of the workhouse gates. He had drawn her to a stop and now, peering at her in the light of the distant street-lamp, he said, 'How d'you feel?'

'I couldn't tell you, Fred, because . . . because I've never felt like this before in me life.'

'I'm coming in with you,' he said, 'but . . . but I just want a last word. I just want to say I promise you you'll never regret it. There'll be some tough times ahead, especially from my lot. Yours, I don't think, will bother you.

'Anyway, as I said, the people will be out of the flat on Monday. I'll get it cleaned up at nights because from what I saw they weren't very spruce, and I'll try to get some bits and pieces in it by next weekend. There's one good thing, the river'll be between our lot and us: I thought it best to go to the north side. You're cold.'

He put his hand out and touched her cheek, and she said, 'No, no, I'm not, Fred. I'm warm. I'm so warm I know I'll never feel cold again. And, Fred, I want to say something too.' There followed a few seconds of silence before she went on. 'I – I never knew until today what love was. But I know this, and – and with certainty, that I love you and I'll never stop loving you. There'll be rough and smooth, as you say, but until the day I die I'll be grateful to you.'

At half past eleven that morning their lips had met for the first time in a perfunctory and shy kiss. Now their arms were about each other, their bodies close. When at last they parted neither of them spoke but, as of one mind, they turned towards the gate and went in.

'Where's that girl? I want to talk to her.'

A week had passed and Mary Ryan looked from her brother to her sister-in-law and said, 'What girl?'

'Don't be daft, our Mary. Don't play games, you know what girl,' said her brother. 'We were against the whole business afore, but since then I've come up with her father . . . My God, what a man! Bigoted crazy ranter, if ever there was one. Our Fred's having nothin' to do with her or that lot; I'll see him dead first. And that's another thing: has he been here the day?'

'I haven't seen him.'

'Well, where's he gone?' It was her sister-in-law speaking now, and Mary looked at her and said, 'How do you think I would know, Chrissy?'

'Because he's always come to you. He's thought more of you than he should, and you've encouraged him, took him away. And you're not good for him. He almost missed his Easter duties, and that was through you and your talk, which he comes out with, saying nobody in this place owes God anything. Dreadful thing to say. Anyway, where's that girl? She's always round here on a Saturday, I'll be bound, hangin' about for him.'

'Well, she isn't around here the day. She's gone out, an' taken the bairn with her.'

'*No. No.*' Chrissy McCall's voice rose to a crescendo as she pressed her outspread hand against her ample breast. 'She's – she hasn't gone with him? No, no, don't tell me that, Mary.'

'Oh, no, she hasn't gone with him, Chrissy, not like that, not just like that, livin' with him like. The fact is, they've gone on their honeymoon, having been married a week. Oh dear me. Dear me.'

Her sister-in-law had slumped against her

husband; and when her brother put in, in a small voice, 'Married? They couldn't. They've never been to ch—' Mary laughed.

'Oh, you haven't necessarily to go to church to get married, Patrick. You should know that by now. No: they did it in the register office last Saturday morning. They had the day off.'

'*Oh, Holy Mary.*'

When Chrissy McCall slid from her husband's grasp to her knees, seemingly oblivious of the interest she was causing in the day room, her husband cried, 'Get up, woman.' He hauled her to her feet by the shoulder of her coat, and pushed her towards the ward door. But there he stopped and, pointing a finger at his sister, he cried, 'You're at the bottom of this! You egged him on to marry the daughter of a ranter and her with a bastard. I'll never forgive you as long as I live. Neither will God. No! Neither will God.'

After their departure the room was quiet. Then Mary, no smile on her face now, muttered to Susan Ridley, 'Saturdays will never be the same again. Life will go back to what it was in the beginning, is now, and ever shall be.' Then she added thoughtfully, 'I wonder how long the lass will be able to hold out against the lot of them. Anyway, if they don't have her they'll have the bairn and those that will come because Fred's conscience will be at work by then.' She gave a sad little laugh. 'Suffer little children as long as they come in by way of the church service, be it Catholic or Protestant or what-have-you. What do you bet, Susan, that before another arrives they'll have that lass at the altar rails? Although, mind, I think Sally would be strong enough to stick out against white. Don't you?'

When they laughed together there was no gaiety threaded through it. Then they became silent while they looked round the day room and into their inevitable future: it was as if one had lost a son, the other a daughter, for Fred had been the only son Mary had known and, for a year, Sally had come to be like a daughter to Susan Ridley. It was she now who said, 'But they promised to visit, faithfully, they did. As Fred said, hell and high water or a string of bairns won't ever alter their Saturdays.'

'You're right, Susan, you're right.'

They smiled at each other.

It was her friend's gasp that caused Mary to turn her head towards the ward door, there to see standing the lass and Fred, with the child in his arms, and the child, too, was smiling.

Mary's mouth opened wide, but she could find no words until they were standing before them, when Fred said, 'We waited until me ma and da went 'cos we didn't want the war to start in here.'

'But – but this is your special day, we didn't expect you.'

It was Sally now who said, 'We promised to visit every Saturday, so here we are. And you know something?' She gripped a hand of each of them. 'I just said to Fred as we came through those gates, I must be the only person in the whole wide world to say, "God bless the workhouse"!'

3

The Forbidden Word

1953

Owen Evans didn't hurry from the pit head. He'd had his bath, got into his clean suit, then stood in the yard and looked up at the heavens. Having seen it was a fine bright morning, he had decided to take a stroll through the fields before he returned to the village, the empty house, and bed.

He didn't care for this shift because, by the time he reached home, his mother had left for her job in the store, and even with long practice he found it difficult to sleep through the day.

His home was the last but one in the long row that eased its way up the hill. He let himself in at the front door and went along the passage straight into the kitchen. His breakfast was set out as usual: three slices of bacon in the pan, two eggs and two sausages by the side of it, and five slices of thick bread stacked on the breadboard at the end of the table.

He stood in his shirtsleeves at the sink filling the kettle, looking out of the window over the low railings that separated the two small gardens, and screwed up his face as he watched Bonny, the Joneses' dog, scratching at the back door. Now, that was funny, because the dog was as used to the routine of the Joneses' life as he was to his own. Twelve years old and run to fat, she was content to spend most of her days in the kennel at the bottom of the garden, and had long ceased to bark at Morgan the postie, or the English fellow, Smith the milk. So neither Myfanwy nor Hugh Jones was at home. Something must be wrong, because only last night they had returned from their holidays in Llandudno. Full of beans they were, bragging about their son David's house and his brand new car, and what they thought of him in the chapel. But now there must be somebody else in the house or that dog wouldn't be pawing at the door.

He looked towards a hook on the wall to the side of the sink. The Joneses always left the spare key with them when they went on holiday so that Owen's mother could see to the budgie and the goldfish. They were usually very smarmy when they wanted a good turn done, those two, but in between they were a little too big for their boots.

The key was still there. With all the talk last night his mother had forgotten to pass it back to them. He decided he'd better have a look.

He went out by the back door, stepped over the railings and, bending down, patted the dog's head. 'What's up, Bonny? Burglars?' he said. Then he answered himself: 'Well, that isn't unknown. They might think they're still away – it gets round.'

In the Joneses' kitchen, he again screwed up his

face. Now, that was funny: there was no sign of the breakfast having been set. Three dirty teacups were on the draining-board, and the tea caddy had been left in the middle of the table. Myfanwy Jones and his mother had been in competition for years as to who kept the brightest and most orderly house. Everything was done according to a rota. But whatever had happened here this morning it had been a rush job.

He looked around. Where had the dog gone? He went out of the kitchen, into the passage, and saw Bonny coming from the sitting room. Then she stood at the foot of the stairs and looked up before she began to pull herself towards him step by step.

Good Lord! That dog knew there was somebody up there. Likely Myfanwy had taken bad.

He took the narrow stairs two at a time. The dog was scratching at one of the bedroom doors and so, without hesitation, he went to open it. It was locked but the key was there. Slowly he turned it, then pushed the door wide before stepping into the room then standing stock still.

The dog had lifted herself up and placed her front paws on the knees of a young girl sitting on the side of the bed. Bonny's head reached up to her and the girl was stroking her but looking towards the man standing in the doorway.

He had seen Gwen Jones only twice since she had left the valley to go to that fancy art school. On both occasions her mother had guarded her as if he himself were a mad dog ready to pounce on her daughter. Myfanwy and Hugh Jones had bigger ideas for their daughter: not only had she a voice like a lark but, as her mother was fond of saying, she could paint like nobody's business. And she had been painting like nobody's business for over a year now.

'Hello, Owen.'

'My God!'

She pushed the dog's paws down, slid off the bed, then said, 'What did you say, Owen? My God? You did, didn't you? And you're gaping. You always gaped when you were surprised. If I remember, the last time I surprised you was when I swore, using two naughty words – not one, two. Tut, tut! Little Gwen Jones knowing such words when on a Sunday she sang solo in the chapel and looked like an angel.'

'Oh, Gwen. My God! How could you?'

On this question she pursed her lips, put her hand on the large mound of her stomach, then said, 'Those are the exact words that Dad used last night. But, as I said to him, it was easy and enjoyable.'

'*Shut up!* You're talking like a trollop.'

Her expression altered, and her body stiffened. 'Don't you use that tone to me, Owen Evans, or call me by that name. If I'm a trollop I'm in good company in some quarters of the chapel. And you can substantiate that, can't you, Owen? You didn't want the young birds, they weren't experienced enough. Anyway, an excursion into that quarter might have tied you up for life. Marriage wasn't for you, a free-lancer. Even when you began to notice me you wouldn't come forward.'

'Your mother saw to that.'

'If you'd had any guts you could have got over that. Anyway, here I am back in the old homestead and locked in before I'm packed off to London to Aunt Phyllis's. Mam's gone to phone her now. The last time I saw Aunt Phyllis was when I was seven years old. She wasn't considered good company then, but now she's Mam and Dad's only hope of saving face. You see, nobody knows I'm here. I got a lift in on a lorry last night and arrived around midnight. If your mam wasn't such a heavy sleeper after taking her secret bottle of stout, she would have heard the hullabaloo. Of course, that didn't go on for very long. Anyway, if the unknown Aunt Phyllis will give me house room I'm to be shipped off to her tonight – in the dark, of course. I couldn't leave by the station, now, could I? Dad means to drive me half-way. And I said to them, "What if I don't turn up at Aunt Phyllis's and decide to come back here instead?" And you know what my dear parents said to me, Owen Evans? Practically in one voice they said, "You wouldn't do that to us, would you, Gwen, not that?"'

He watched her face crinkle as if she was about to cry, but she wiped her hand across her mouth instead. The action was very much that of a man, not of a nineteen-year-old girl, even though at this moment she appeared to him to be a fully fledged woman. He watched her push the dog aside, then walk towards the window, only to stop and say, in a low, broken tone, 'I forgot. I promised her not to look out of the window.'

He said now, 'You couldn't get away from the valley quick enough, could you? It was too narrow for you.'

She glanced at him. 'It still is.'

There was silence between them for some seconds before he asked, 'Couldn't he have married you?'

'Oh!' She swung round now, her arms extended, her fingers spread wide as if pressing him away. 'You're like everything and everyone in this dead hole, you never change, you still ask the stupidest questions. Do you think I'd be standing here looking into your shocked face if I could have been married? He was like you in a way, frightened of the death he'd never die, frightened of being tied. He got a sudden call and went abroad. Anyway, I know now I couldn't have stood him day in and day out like the women of this village have to stand you men. When the urge is fulfilled, what's left? Work of one kind or another and the chapel. Oh, yes, the chapel, the hub of life that is oiled by the silver voices of the choir.'

'You can't blame the chapel for what's become of you.'

'Well, I do, and the hymn-singing lot of you. What has the chapel done for any of you but make you afraid of what one will say of the other – me, for instance. As Dad said, his good-living life has gone for nothing all because of me, for now he wouldn't be able to lift up his head again if it became known what I'd sunk to.'

At the sound of footsteps on the stairs, they both turned and looked towards the open door. It was

Myfanwy Jones who gaped now, at Owen Evans, and muttered, '*Oh, no! No!*'

'Yes, yes, Mam. Dad's always said you shouldn't leave the keys next door for them to go poking round. You should have asked them if you could take the budgie and the goldfish over there.'

Owen felt himself taken by the shoulders and pushed out of the room. Then he heard the door slammed and locked. Now she was forcing him downstairs and into the kitchen. There, her hands joined tightly in front of her grey tweed coat, Myfanwy Jones whimpered, 'Owen, Owen, can you believe it? It'll be the death of us. But, please, Owen, I beg you, in the name of the Lord, to keep this to yourself. Now, will you? Will you? Don't breathe a word of it. Not even to your mother. Oh, no, not to Olwyn, because she couldn't keep it to herself. I'm sorry to say this, Owen, but you know what I mean.'

'It's all right, it's all right. Don't worry, I won't let on.'

'You promise? Her dad would die. He's in a state, he's frantic.'

He said, 'She's almost on her time, I would say. Didn't you know? She was here three months ago.'

'No. We were fools. She said she was putting on weight, and she wore one of the modern sack dress things. And who would think my Gwen would do a thing like that after the way she's been brought up, Owen, I ask you?'

'Aye, after the way she's been brought up.' He turned from her now and made for the door, and she followed him, begging again, 'You won't, will you? You won't let on?'

For answer, he said, 'Have you fixed her up in London?'

'Yes, yes. Phyllis seemed very agreeable. She has a boarding-house, you know. I've never been there, because . . . well, she and I were never close. She's different from me.'

'Yes.' He nodded at her. Yes, she would be.

He went out now, got over the fence, pushed open the kitchen door, closed it behind him, then stood with his back to it, his eyes closed.

It was four months later when he said to his mother, 'What would you say, Mam, if I told you I was thinking about asking Gwen Jones to marry me?'

'What would I say?' Olwyn Evans looked at her son, then laughed. 'Have you forgotten the two mountains beyond the railings? You'd have to climb them before you got at their daughter. And anyway, from what I hear from Myfanwy she's in London now and apparently doing well, so well that she doesn't bother to come home. What I don't understand is the way Olwyn took the news of the girl leaving the college, and after only a year of the three-year course they used to brag about. I sometimes think I smell a rat. So you ask what would I say if you wanted to marry her? Well, it's up to you, that's all. She was always a decent enough girl as far as I recall, in spite of being smothered by them two. I was amazed when they decided to let her off the leash and go to that college, especially him, because, you know, he used to act as if she were God's adopted daughter. As I once said to your dad, may he rest in peace, if they had been Catholics, like the Learys across the road, he would have had her into a convent and a chastity belt on her.'

He laughed now as he said, 'Oh, I don't think the Romans go as far as the belt.'

'Well, the habit is as good as, isn't it?' his mother replied.

He let another two weeks go by before he stepped over the railings on a Saturday afternoon and surprised Hugh Jones. 'Could I have a private word with you and Myfanwy, Hugh?'

'Yes, of course, lad. But what could be so private that you have to ask if you can speak it? Come into the front room and sit yourself down.'

He sat opposite the pair of them. Then, after a moment, he said, 'I won't beat about the bush. It's about Gwen.'

When he saw Myfanwy Jones's mouth open and close twice, he went on, 'I was wondering if you'd object to me as a son-in-law.'

He watched them exchange glances. Myfanwy spoke first. 'For my part, Owen, I'd welcome you. Yes, I would, I'd welcome you. What about you, Dad?' She turned and looked at her husband, and Hugh Jones, nodding now, said, 'We've always known you as a God-fearing young man, Owen, and I would be pleased to welcome you as a son-in-law.'

Owen smiled now from one to the other, then said, 'Well, it's up to me now to go and see Gwen and ask her how she views the proposition, isn't it?'

'Yes.' They answered together.

'Is she still with her auntie?'

'Yes.'

He was confirming what he had previously heard from Myfanwy. He'd also been told that the baby, a boy child, had been adopted; and that she had found work in the city. What kind of work, however, had not been made clear. Apparently she was a kind of receptionist. And this, he thought, was a pity, because that wouldn't give her much scope for her art. However, here he was, sitting opposite these two stiff-necks, as he had always thought of them, and they were telling him that they would welcome him as a son-in-law. Well, now, he would see.

'I'll go up next weekend,' he said, and added, 'Don't tell her I'm coming. I don't want her to scarper with fright.' And he laughed.

He left the valley early on the Saturday morning. An hour later he took the train from Cardiff station to London. He was wearing his best suit and carrying a light mackintosh, and a ginger cake. He arrived in London at a quarter to one, and at half past a taxi put him down in a terrace on the outskirts of Ealing. He found himself outside quite a big house, with three storeys, topped by an attic window. He rang the bell and was presently admitted. An hour later he left, walked some distance until he found a taxi and asked for Hyde Park. There, he walked for some time before making his way back to

Paddington station. He was fortunate to board a train that was due to leave fifteen minutes later for Cardiff.

He got out of the train at nine o'clock, and caught a bus that dropped him off at the bottom of the hill. He did not go to his own home, but knocked on the Joneses' front door. It was opened by Myfanwy who peered at him, then exclaimed, 'Oh, 'tis Owen. And you're back early, boy. Come in, come in. Your mother's here. We were just talking.'

He passed her without a word, walked along the passage and into the front room. Hugh Jones and his mother were standing, and Hugh repeated his wife's words: 'You're back early.'

Owen still did not speak, until his mother asked quietly, 'You had a good trip, boy?'

Then he said, his voice high as if he was about to burst into song, 'Oh, yes, Mam, splendid trip, splendid.'

He was smiling now but his lips were closed tightly, and he nodded as he looked from one to the other. Myfanwy asked, in a small voice, 'You saw Gwen?'

'Oh, yes, Mrs Jones. I saw Gwen.'

He had called her Mrs Jones, not Myfanwy or Auntie as he used to do when he was a boy.

'She's all right?' The question this time came from Hugh, and Owen, looking him full in the face, said, 'Yes, yes, she's all right, splendid.'

'Oh, that's good. Sit down.'

'No, thank you, Mr Jones. I've had a longish journey, there and back, and I'd like to get me feet up.'

'But – but what about . . . well, the purpose of your journey?' Myfanwy was bending towards him now. 'Did you . . . did you find her comfortable? I mean, what was our Phyllis's house like?'

'Oh, that. Splendid, a splendid house. Oh, yes.' He sucked in his breath. 'Never seen finer.'

'It's a guest-house, then, as she said?'

'Yes, it's a guest-house.'

'Then she has company . . . Gwen?'

'She has that, Mr Jones. Yes, she has that, and all smart and well set-up. And she sends you a message.' He drew a deep breath, then let it out before he said, 'She says to thank you for her present position. She would never have found such a one here in the valley. And that's true.'

'She's . . . she's happy, then?' There was a perplexed expression on Hugh Jones's face.

'Happy? As gay as a lark.' And now he turned and looked at Myfanwy. 'And your sister sent a message for you too. She said you're welcome any time you'd like to go up.'

His mother broke in now, sounding strained: 'Owen, you made the journey for one reason. Did you put the question to her?'

'Put the question to her, Mam?' He drew himself up and squared his shoulders. 'No bloody fear. Me put the question to a whore in a brothel? Come on.' He put out his hand towards her. 'Let's leave Mr and Mrs Jones to think over which would have been the lesser of two evils: to have the valley know that they had a daughter who had a bairn, likely through ignorance owing to them caging her, or one who had turned into a prostitute. Still, they can be proud that she's risen in the world, in the profession that she's chosen, because she's no common street-walker. No, she has her own set of rooms, which no ordinary fellow in the valley or anyone like me could have provided for her.'

He pressed his mother through into the passage, but paused and looked back at the couple, who were transfixed with horror. And he said, slowly and grimly, 'You won't be going to the chapel tomorrow now, will you, Mr Jones? I'd advise you not to, 'cos I'll have the urge to spit on you in public. And you too, Mrs Jones, for I think you're more to blame than him because you knew your sister wasn't much good years ago. Yet, you could sacrifice your daughter to her to save your face. And another thing: if you take my advice you'll suddenly have an urge to move – and why not to London? When you asked me some months ago to keep me mouth shut, you said it would be better if me mam here didn't know, for it was an impossibility for her to keep hers shut. And I agree with you . . . Me mam's a blabber.'

A few minutes later, standing in their own kitchen, Olwyn looked at him and asked quietly, 'Was all that true?' He nodded. Then, after a moment's silence, she said, 'Well, if you want to know what I think, Owen, I think in spite of all you should have asked her – my God, I think you should – and got her out of that place.'

He stared back at her, then said, 'I did, Mam. I made me offer but she refused it.'

'She did, boy?'

'Aye, she did.'

'Oh, well, if that's the case she likely laughed at you for being such a bloody fool.'

'No, she didn't, Mam, she cried.'

4

The Forbidden Word

1983

'I love you, Steve.'

'And I love you, Susie.'

'What are we going to do?'

The young fellow shook his head and stared out from the bus shelter into the pouring rain; after a moment, he said, 'It's funny, isn't it, your mother for you and your father not, and my dad for me and me mum dead against the idea?' Then, on a tight laugh, he added, 'If your mother and my dad could get together that would simplify matters. We could live with them, couldn't we?'

She leant her head against his shoulder and he pressed her tightly to him as he ended, 'It's a sure thing we can't live in either house as things are.'

She turned her face up towards him. Then withdrawing herself from his arm, she turned up the collar of her coat. 'Why do they take all the fun out of life, all the joy?' She looked at him again, and endeavouring to focus on his face in the light from the street-lamp, she said, 'You know, you never hear people speaking that word, do you, "joy"? And it's been in the back of my mind for years, wondering really what joy would feel like. I remember my grandfather saying something about my father. "He's my son," he said, "but he's never known joy." Funny that, isn't it?'

Taking her wet face between his hands, he said, 'You're my joy and my love,' but then, his tone flippant, he added, 'and my Hot Lips.'

'Oh, you, Steve Roperly – Hot Lips!'

'Well, you are like her. Every time I look at *M.A.S.H.* I see you – only, of course, half her age.'

'Thank you.'

Their arms tight around each other, they kissed; and a woman, coming into the shelter, said, 'My goodness me!'

Drawing apart, they looked at her for a moment, then stepped out into the street. They had gone a few yards when they both giggled and mimicked, 'My goodness me!'

Close together, their heads down, they hurried along the rainswept promenade. Then, fifteen minutes later, while they were saying their last goodnight, he asked quietly, 'When are you going to tell them about it?'

'As soon as I get in. What about you?'

'I'll do the same.'

'Look, I've hardly got in the house and I've had a hard day. I'm fighting for my life in that office and I can't get through this indifferent meal before you start. Well, I'll give you the answer now, it's the same as I gave you last night: they can come for the weekend, but there's two spare bedrooms upstairs and they'll use them both. God almighty! What kind of a woman are you even to consider your daughter lying next door and having it off with a man she's not even engaged to and, as she plainly says, she's not going to marry? Talk about immorality, you're condoning dirt, pornographic—'

'Shut up!' Betty Heedman banged her knife and fork down at each side of her plate and, thrusting her face across the table towards her husband, she cried, 'You talk like your mother used to. She was a narrow, ignorant slob of a woman. She had to wait until she was forty-four before she had you, and that was a mistake.' And she sprang up from the table, leaving her husband gripping the edge of it, his face livid. With her back against the draining-board she growled, under her breath, 'I've got nothing in my life but her, and I'm not going to lose her. And I'll tell you something, Mr Sanctimonious Heedman, he's not only coming for the weekend, soon he'll be coming to stay, both her and him . . . She's pregnant.'

She watched her husband rise slowly from his chair but instead of the expected explosion he stammered, 'Pr-pr-pregnant? No! No! Wh-wh-what about the pills you insisted on her t-t-taking?'

'She decided not to take them. She wanted a baby.'

'*Oh, my God!*' He put his hands to his head now and walked in a tight circle then stopped suddenly and yelled at her, 'Frank! What impression is this going to make on Frank, and him still at school?'

For some seconds she did not answer him, and then, although her voice held a sneer, it was also threaded with a trace of pity as she said, 'Oh, John, I sometimes think your mind got stuck somewhere in your childhood. This is nineteen eighty-three, not the fifties. Our Frank's sixteen, and he's been at it for some time now with that sweet little Joanie next door, the "little girl" you still pat on the head.'

Turning now to the sink, she washed her hands, then dried them on a tea-towel, which she threw on to the draining-board. Looking at him, as he stood at the other side of the table, his jaws tight, his hands clenched by his sides, she said quietly, 'It's a pity your mother died when she did because then you would never have married. And, oh, what a different life I might have had.' On this she went quietly from the kitchen.

When the door swung closed, he stared towards it for a moment then sat down at the table again, and beat his fists rhythmically on the surface, staring at his wife's half-finished meal as it bounced slightly with each thump towards the edge. When it toppled off, his hands stilled, he sat back in his chair and drew a long, shuddering breath. It was as if, in his mind, he had felled her to the floor.

'Oh, I can understand your attitude.' Sheila Roperly pursed her lips and nodded as she stared down at her husband slumped in the corner of the couch staring at the blank television screen. 'Like father, like son, and definitely in this case! What should I expect but—'

'Now, stop it, Sheila.' He had pulled himself upright and, his arm thrust out now, his forefinger wagging at her, he went on, 'You bring that up again and we'll go back to the beginning and find out why I supposedly went off the rails. That was purely your imagination. There never was anyone, you just wanted to put the blame on me. But stick to the point.'

Sam Roperly got to his feet now and looked at the plump figure of his wife. 'That's what we must do, stick to the point, and the point is this: loosen your apron strings, get him off your knee, let him go. He's not a bairn any longer, hasn't been for a long time, but you've closed your eyes to it. And I'll tell you something else you've closed your eyes to an' all. He's resented being coddled . . . "Where's my boy?"' He was imitating her voice now, twisting his face into a weird smile. Then, his tone grim again, he went on, 'He's not a boy, he's a young man of twenty. And Sheila,' he bent towards her, and his words came slow and emphatically, 'he's got a girl. He's living with her. It's here and there, wherever the opportunity offers, and what he wants now is to bring her home for the weekend—'

'*Not in my house.*' Her small body bristled. 'Oh, you!' She moved her head from one side to the other and her lips trembled as she muttered, 'You could lie in bed and know that your son was next door.' She closed her eyes on the scene her words presented to her. Then, stretching her small frame upwards, she cried, 'They're not going to use my house as a brothel. Let them get married and then we'll see.'

She was making for the door when he said quietly, 'He has no intention of marrying, nor, from what I understand, has she. But I've got news for you, Sheila . . . She's pregnant.'

She'd had her hand on the knob of the sitting-room door and had partly opened it. When it banged closed the sound was like a shot from a gun. And it seemed that his last word had caused an explosion in her, for in swinging round to face him again she appeared to leave the ground, and her voice spiralled up: 'What? What did you say?'

'You heard.'

She gulped and cried, 'Trapped! She's trapped him.'

'Don't be silly, woman. In any case, if there's been any trapping done, likely it's come from his side.'

'Don't *you* be silly, Sam Roperly. Girls like her are on the pill; some of them are at it from school-days. I've seen her. I know her type, all bust and backside.'

'Huh!' He laughed now. 'Look who's talking about bust and backside. Still, there's a difference between you, seeing that she can give you a good foot in height. She's a nice tall lass.'

'You're enjoying this, aren't you, Sam?' Her voice was a thin whisper. 'In a way you're getting your own back on me through him, aren't you? If you can't get all you want you're going to see that he does. Well, if it's the last thing I do, I'll put a stop to it. I'll see her folks. I'll tell them she's not coming here and he's not going there.'

'Do that, Sheila. But what if they're sensible people and don't want to lose their daughter and they say to our Stephen, "You're welcome, lad. We don't mind you sleeping next door with our lass and making love, 'cos it's the most natural thing in the world"? And they might add, "I'm glad times have changed, because we had to get married before we could look at our bare skin."'

'You! You've got a filthy mind.'

'Well, if I have, my son takes after me. Just think on that, Sheila. My son takes after me.'

When the door banged he put his hand to his head and ran his fingers through his thick, greying hair, then sat down on the corner of the couch again and stared at the blank television screen.

She was standing at the bus shelter again, out of the rain, waiting, when the car drew up alongside the kerb and Stephen's hand came out, beckoning her towards him.

She was leaning in at the window now, asking, 'Where have you got this?'

'I stole it. Come on, quick, get in, you're wet.'

As she took her seat beside him, he said, 'I'm delivering it to Mrs Neilson, Brooker Terrace . . . Hello, love.'

'Hello, you,' she answered, then added, 'Is that the woman who had the break-in?'

'Yes, the same one. And the boss is worried about her. She's his favourite customer and her husband before her.'

'Her husband's dead, then?'

'Yes. And not only him but her son and daughter, all within six years of each other, so I understand from the boss. Her husband dropped down dead and him just in his late fifties. Two years later her only daughter died in childbirth. The last one to go was her son. His car went into a wall on an icy bend. He was about thirty and single. And there she's been, left on her own these last two years. But apparently, so the boss says, she didn't mind until the break-in, and the mess they left. She's advertising now for a gardener-handyman to live in.' He glanced at her, grinning now, as he said, 'It's a pity I don't know one end of a shovel from the other. But even if I did, I'd hate the idea of gardening. And as for handyman! Huh!' He laughed. 'It's funny, you know, I can take the inside out of a car, treat every nut, screw and bolt gently, I even stroke the wires, but a bull in a china shop would be more use than I would be in a house. I take after Dad – he's even worse.'

'Is it a big house?' she asked.

'Well, you know Brooker Grove, it's round the corner from the garage.'

'Oh, there! They are biggish houses, all semi-detached.'

'Hers isn't. It's at the end and it's got the garden on three sides of it. The front part's cleared, but the back's like a wilderness.'

When he turned into the drive and stopped the car, she said, 'Can I come in with you?'

'No reason why not.'

After Stephen had knocked on the door it was opened to the length of the safety-chain, and he said, 'It's me, Mrs Neilson, Stephen Roperly from the garage. I've brought the car.'

'Oh.' The door was pulled wide and a smartly dressed woman looked from one to the other. 'I . . . I have to be careful. Won't you come in a minute?'

She closed and locked the hall door behind them, then said, 'I was in the kitchen. I've just made some coffee, would you care for a cup?'

They both spoke at once. 'Yes, please, thank you.' Then they laughed, and she laughed too.

The kitchen was warm from the Aga and Stephen remarked, 'It's cosy in here.' Pointing to the Aga, he said, 'They give off a good heat, don't they?'

'Especially in the night when I come down . . . I don't sleep well,' she replied.

She brought two fine china cups from a cupboard, then took the percolator from the side of the stove and poured the coffee. As she motioned them to the chairs around the table, she said, 'Do sit down,' and added, 'Since those hooligans broke in, I've hardly slept at all.'

She was seated at the table now and when she spoke again, it was more to herself: looking down into the cup of steaming coffee, she said, 'Odd, but I didn't mind being alone before, I felt they were still here, my . . . my family.' She looked across the table from one young face to the other. 'I lost them, you see.'

75

'Yes, I know.' Stephen nodded sympathetically.

She stirred her coffee vigorously. 'I've – I've advertised for a gardener-handyman, to live in, of course. It will be very difficult because most men are married – at least, those who would fit the post.'

'Oh, you're bound to get someone,' Stephen said. 'I'd take it myself, only it's not an exaggeration to say that I hate gardening. And my efforts inside the house would be along similar lines to those who broke in.'

Her smile was broad now as she said, 'Oh, I don't believe that. You're so very good with the car.'

'Well, I was just saying to Susie here, coming along, I've got a kind of surgeon's hands inside the body of a car, but when it comes to doing anything in the house, my mother won't let me near a hammer or a nail. I don't know what will happen when we set up home.'

'Are you engaged?'

They glanced at each other, and it was Susan who answered: 'Not like that, no rings or anything, but we are promised to each other. We . . . we know what we want.'

'Well,' Mrs Neilson sighed, 'that is the modern outlook, and I'm sure you can't do much worse with your lives than some of the married couples hereabouts.'

'No, we've thought that too.'

A silence followed, and when it became embarrassing Stephen said, 'Shall I put the car in the garage for you?'

'If you would, please. Have you finished your coffee? Would you like another?'

'No, thank you,' they said, together again.

'You can come through the annexe to the garage,' she said, rising from the table. 'It will stop you getting wet.'

They followed her out of the kitchen, through a utility room, then through a door that swung heavily behind them. When she switched on the light, they were in a largish room that held a wooden table, a couch and two chairs, looking the worse for wear. In one corner a number of boxes were stacked one on top of the other, all labelled. But what brought Stephen to a halt were the walls: they were covered with posters and pictures of racing cars. At the door leading from the room Mrs Neilson stopped and looked back at him. In a low voice she said, 'This was my son's . . .' she paused '. . . games room.' Then she looked at Susan before she pushed open another door. 'And my daughter used this one.'

They walked into the second room. It wasn't quite so large, and under one window there was a sink with a bench attached. On it were boxes of tools. Again Mrs Neilson paused before she said, 'My daughter used to model and sculpt.'

Quickly now she opened the door that led into the yard, and Stephen said, 'Don't come out. Stay out of the rain. I'll bring it round.'

Mrs Neilson stepped back into the room and, looking about her, she murmured, 'This used to be the cook-housekeeper's quarters in my husband's early days. I'll have to have it cleaned up.' Then, looking at Susan, she went on, 'For the man who's going to take the post, you know.' She smiled now. 'It's a pity your young man doesn't like gardening and isn't handy in the house.'

Susan sighed, then said, in a voice apparently weighed down with regret, 'Yes, it is, isn't it?'

'He's such a nice young man, so pleasant. He's always so helpful when I go to the garage.'

Susan gave no answer to this, only smiled. Then they stood listening to the car being driven into the garage, and the door being pulled down.

When Stephen joined them he stood for a moment in the open doorway shaking the wet from his hair; then he peered up at a board nailed across the top of the door. Letters had been burnt into it, but although the board itself stood out against the dirty white paint on the door, the letters were difficult to make out. Presently, he stepped further into the room and, looking at Mrs Neilson, he smiled broadly at her while thumbing towards the board and saying, 'Timbuktu? Am I right, is that what it says?'

'Yes, Timbuktu. My son was just a boy when he put it there. He always said he would go to faraway places, and he did – he travelled the world, racing.' She stepped forward, looked at the board and said softly, 'Whenever he was abroad he would send a card, saying, "Back in Timbuktu at such and such a time."'

In the kitchen again Mrs Neilson looked from

one to the other, asking, 'Sure you wouldn't like another cup of coffee?'

Stephen began, 'No, thanks, we must get back,' but Susan put in, 'I wouldn't mind one, please. It was very nice coffee, different. I'm used to Nescafé.'

Half an hour later they left the house and as they walked along the terrace, heads down against the rain, Stephen said, 'They'll be wondering where you are. They'll have the bellman out.'

Susan made no reply, but after a short silence she said, 'She's very lonely – I felt sorry for her. And she's frightened to be there on her own. She must be in her early sixties but she's very smart.' She sighed, then said, 'Why can't you be interested in gardening and handy in the house?'

For answer he pulled her arm closer to him, saying, 'Well, you know what you're taking on. And I can tell you this, no matter what kind of a place we get in the future, it won't have a garden if I have anything to do with it.'

When they reached the end of the terrace, she said, 'Look, I'm going to get the bus. You're not coming all that way with me, you're soaked.' She pushed him. 'Now, don't start arguing. Anyway, I've got to have time to think, to fortify myself. And here's a bus coming.'

After they had kissed, she said, 'I'll give you a ring tomorrow at work.'

'Good night, love,' he said, and kissed her again.

The bus driver opened the automatic doors and shouted, 'Enough of that now! Enough of that!'

As Susan passed him, she grinned. 'Jealous?'

He grinned back at her. 'You could say.'

The following lunchtime when Susan phoned the garage, she started to speak abruptly: 'You know what the latest is? Your mother and father are coming round to our place on Friday night to discuss us and the future.'

'*No*. When did this happen?'

'Yesterday, apparently. You didn't know?'

'Not a word, although now you come to mention it, Dad wanted to say something to me last night when I came in, but Mum shut him up.'

'Stephen.'

'Yes, love?'

'I . . . I may be a little late at the bus shelter tonight, even as much as half an hour. It's a stocktaking.'

'All right, love. 'Bye.'

She was almost three-quarters of an hour late arriving at the bus shelter, and she did not appear as she usually did, on foot, but got off a bus on the opposite side of the road. He went to meet her, and even in the fading light he saw that her eyes were shining, her whole face was bright. She looked beautiful. 'What's up?' he said. 'Where've you been? Why have you come by bus?'

She took his arm, then said, 'Let's walk along the front, I've got something to tell you.'

The night was warm; the moon was coming up over the sea; it had been a fine day, following a week of rain. She flung out an arm and pointed out to sea, saying, 'I'm over that.'

'Over what? What d'you mean?'

'Over the moon.'

He pulled her to a stop. 'What is it? What's happened?'

'I'll tell you what's happened.' She took his arm, and as they walked on she talked. Three times he stopped, and three times she pulled him forward. The fourth time he took her into his arms and hugged her and, their heads together, they laughed.

On the Friday night he drew the car up to the kerb opposite the bus station, and when she got in they grinned at each other. 'Did you manage?' she asked.

'Yes, it's all in the back there.' He jerked his head towards the boot. 'How about you?'

'I went back at dinnertime. She always has her hair done on a Friday, but she was there.'

'Oh, Lord! What did she say?'

'She was for us. Sort of sad. Anyway, she's not going to say anything until we arrive. Funny, but I think she's going to enjoy it, like getting one back on him . . . Father. Don't let us ever get like that, Stephen.'

He took one hand off the wheel and gripped hers for a moment, then said, 'I won't, because we'll talk it out.'

She leant her head against his arm, and he said, 'Look out! I'm a responsible driver.'

'Will you be a responsible husband?'

'Yes, as long as you're a responsible wife, I'll be that . . . between rows.' They laughed.

When he stopped the car outside her home they both sighed, looked at each other and, as they had become apt to do, they spoke together. 'Now for it.'

On the pavement they gripped hands, then opened the iron gate between the trim hedges, went up the garden path, round the side of the house and into the kitchen.

It was empty but the sound of voices came to them from the sitting room. And when John Heedman's precise tones took over, Susan closed her eyes and lowered her head as she muttered, 'He's got the floor.'

Stephen put his arm around her shoulders and pressed her to him for a moment, saying, 'Well, let's get a better seat and hear what he's got to say.'

John Heedman wasn't surprised to see his daughter; he was, however, not only surprised but angered to see her companion. He glared at the young man and demanded, 'What do you want here?'

At this Sam Roperly, who had been sitting stiffly on the chintz-covered sofa, pulled himself to the front of it, and almost growled, 'He happens to be my son, and he's the reason for our visit, isn't he?'

'Sit down!' Betty Heedman's voice was a command, and her husband rounded on her, his mouth open, but something in her look caused him not to speak his thoughts. He almost flung himself across the room, but he did not sit down: he stood by the mantelpiece, his forearm resting on it, his gaze directed at the artificial logs of the electric fire.

Sam Roperly, now looking at the young couple, said, 'Hello there, son. Hello, Susie.'

Stephen did not answer his father, but Susan said, 'Hello, Mr Roperly.'

And Betty Heedman, looking at Stephen, said, 'Well, come and sit down. Would you like a cup of tea?'

'No, thanks, Mrs Heedman, we're not staying. And I must say straight away I don't think there's any need for discussion about whose house we'll spend the weekend at, ever.'

No-one spoke, but four pairs of eyes turned in their direction.

'What d'you mean?' Sam got to his feet.

'Well, it's like this, Dad, we've got fixed up. Gardener-handyman, with apartment.'

'*What?* Gardener? Handyman?' It was the first time Sheila Roperly had spoken. Until now she had let her eyes and her grim mouth express her feelings, but she was laughing now, a false, high-pitched laugh. 'That's the funniest joke I've heard in years! You? Gardener-handyman? We've never had a garden – you've lived in a flat all your life. You let the window-box die when we went away last year. As for handyman – my God, you're about as handy in the house as he is.' She thumbed now towards her husband. 'You've got a nerve to take such a position. You'll be thrown out on your neck.'

'You're quite right, Mum. I would be thrown out on me neck but, you see, I'm not the gardener-handyman. It's Susie here.'

All eyes were concentrated on Susan, and she smiled now. Speaking directly to her father, she said, 'I've got that much to thank you for, Father. You made me like gardening, although you did it as a punishment, didn't you? Keeping me at it on a Saturday so I wouldn't get a chance to talk to the boys. If you'd guessed I liked it you would have had me locked in my room, wouldn't you? And as for handyman, well, Mum showed me years ago how to mend a fuse and put a washer on a tap. And, if you recall, I decorated my own room and knocked up a bookcase when I was sixteen. Oh, yes, I'm well fitted for the position.'

'You're pregnant.' Sheila Roperly spat the words at her. And Susan replied quietly, 'Yes, Mrs Roperly, I'm pregnant, I'm very pleased to say, and my employer is aware of that and, what's more, she's looking forward to the baby coming. And there's one thing certain, it will never be naked, for she has boxes full of baby clothes left over from her own children.'

'I won't allow it.'

All the attention now was turned on John Heedman. His face was blanched. 'Not . . . not unless you get married,' he added.

As Stephen was about to speak Susan laid a hand gently on his arm and, looking at her father, she said, 'You have no power to stop me doing anything I want to. I was eighteen last week. What you seem to forget, Father, is that's the key-of-the-door age now. And as for being married, we're not going to be married, not until we feel we want to, if ever.'

'What about the child? It'll be illegitimate, a bastard.'

Susan took a step towards her father and her tone held a trace of pity as she said, 'I thought those words would have died for you with Gran. Things are different now. People look at things from quite a different angle. And, anyway, we young ones don't know how many days we have left. In your time you had something to look forward to. What have we got? The promise of extinction. We want to taste this thing called life while we can. Who's going to ask those left on this charred planet if they have marriage lines?'

For a moment, there was utter silence in the room. They all stared at her until her father spluttered, 'That's all propaganda, mob talk. Sin is sin, no matter how you try to cover it. You and your lot, you're selfish. It's all self, self, self. You're not thinking of the child.'

'And you're not thinking of the child either. I know that, Father. Our child will have something that I never had, from you anyway, and that's love.' She flung round and said to Stephen, 'Come on.'

Sam's voice brought her to a halt. 'Do we know where you're bound for, lass?' He moved towards them.

Susan and Stephen turned to each other, then together they said: 'Timbuktu.'

'Oh.' Sam looked puzzled, then asked, 'Where might that be?'

It was Susan who answered. Putting her head

to one side, she looked at her mother. 'Mother knows,' she said. 'She'll bring you.'

Sam Roperly and Betty Heedman looked at each other, and to the further consternation of their respective spouses, Sam smiled broadly at Betty and said, 'That'll be something to look forward to, Mrs Heedman,' and she answered, 'Yes, indeed, it will, Mr Roperly. Timbuktu.'

5

The Creak

It's supposed to be the last straw that breaks the camel's back. But it was something lighter than a straw that broke our camel's back. It was a creak.

Our camel's name is Mabel Campbell and she's going on twenty-six, but looks every day of thirty-six. It was this depressing fact, and the creak, that damaged her back irrevocably. And a good thing too.

Twenty-seven Woodfield Road was a nice house. It was detached and had a whole half-acre of garden to itself. There were five bedrooms, three reception, two baths, a coal-house under cover, but no garage.

In the first year of their marriage Mabel's parents had had a son, whom they named Lionel. Lionel was a quiet baby. He was a well-behaved little boy. And then he was a circumspect youth.

Mabel had come to her parents nine years after Lionel was born, and having got her they had to put up with her. But Mrs Campbell admitted to Mr Campbell that it was such a bother to have to start all this paraphernalia over again when they had the garden to see to, and now that they were just getting into the way of propagating their own rhododendrons and cultivating rare azaleas.

At an early age Mabel sensed that she was in the way, and the only remedy, she realised, was to make herself useful.

As the years went on, Mrs Campbell spent most of her time either in the garden or in the big greenhouse that had recently been built at the bottom of it. After his day in the office – Mr Campbell was a solicitor's clerk – and every weekend, he joined his wife, and they worked assiduously at their joint hobby.

As a child, Mabel thought that her parents were very, very old, but when she was eight and her father died – choked by a bone that wedged in his throat – people said, 'Isn't it a shame, and him only forty-three?'

Mrs Campbell was greatly distressed at the loss of her husband but decided that she must be both mother and father to her son. His career must not suffer. Lionel must be kept at school to prepare himself for the career his father had mapped out for him. Lionel was to be no clerk, he was to be a solicitor. And this would be achieved because both Mr and Mrs Campbell had been gifted with foresight: the foresight to put every penny they could into insurance. This had paid off and because of it, as Mrs Campbell said pointedly to Mabel, if they all pulled in their horns they'd be able to manage.

Pulling in of horns meant no fires until November, and in the summer the thermostat was put on only once a week for baths. Pulling in of horns meant the quick dismissal of Mrs Rogers, who had done the heavy wash on a Monday and gone through the house from top to bottom with lightning speed on a Friday.

'We must all do our bit,' Mrs Campbell also said.

Mabel's seemed quite a large bit. But, then, at eight Mabel looked twelve; she was big-limbed, rather ungainly and distressingly plain. But she was consoled by the fact that she had the asset of all plain people: common sense. Even her mother said she had common sense. She had looked at her one day and remarked, 'Well, if nothing else gets you by, you have your common sense.'

Mabel was twelve when her mother died. She remembered the day well. She was in love with the paper boy and had come downstairs early to catch a glimpse of his long, lugubrious face. After he had warmed her heart by knocking at the door and handing her the newspaper instead of pushing it through the letterbox – this had happened for the past three mornings – she was so elated she decided she would not only set the breakfast but cook it and have it ready for her mother and Lionel when they came downstairs. Lionel came down to breakfast, but not her mother. Mrs Campbell had died during the night. It was found out at the post-mortem that her heart had failed.

Mabel could not understand her reaction to her mother's death. Part of her felt a sense of release that her mother was no longer in the house and would no longer be waiting for her after school with a command, always put over in the form of a request, such as 'Would you like to do so-and-so now, Mabel, or after you've done your homework?' So-and-so might be anything from going to Raine's dairy for the milk – and cracked eggs, if they had any, 'Tell them they're for omelettes' – to doing housework, ironing or weeding.

The feeling of release was almost frighteningly exhilarating, yet side by side with it was a great emptiness. She felt so alone, friendless, almost homeless. And she had been afraid she *was* going to be homeless, until Lionel said, 'I'd do anything not to have to sell this house. They both loved it so much.' She remembered thinking, with the common sense her mother had attributed to her, that it might have been better if they had spread their love around a bit.

And then Lionel had looked at her and said, 'I could keep it. I could manage, just get through with the insurance' – the company had again paid up and looked pleasant about it – 'but it's getting some-body to look after you.'

'Me?' She had reared up until she was nearly as tall as him. 'I don't want anyone to look after me. I can look after myself.' She had almost added, 'I've been doing so for a long time,' but that would have sounded spiteful.

He said, 'Can you? But the housework and the garden?'

'I can do a lot at nights, and we could work in the garden at the weekend.' As she said this, she thought, not with pleasure, It will be like Mother and Father all over again, and the idea repelled her.

But that was how it all started, Mabel's slavery. And now we come to the creak . . .

There had been a creak in the kitchen door from as far back as she could remember. It had first come to her notice when, as a small child, she had stood and watched a man lift it off its hinges, turn it upside down, and rub the bottom with sandpaper. Then she could remember her father tackling the door strategically, determined to ferret out its weak spot. She had watched him move it gently to the right, then quickly to the left. She had watched him shut it with a bang, then close it with the finicky primness of a Victorian lady. She had watched him stand back and look at it with satisfaction after he had drenched it in oil. And when, finally, he had entered the house that night and closed it after him, she had watched him almost reach the ceiling in rage, as the door spoke to him in four tiny consecutive creaks which, interpreted, might have said, 'You can't catch me.'

For long periods at a time the door would behave, or perhaps they got so used to it that they failed to notice its voice. It was when tempers frayed that the door made itself heard. Looking back, Mabel thought it said a lot for the tranquillity of her mind during the three years when she and Lionel managed the house together: hardly once during that time could she remember hearing the door creak.

She was fifteen when Lionel brought Lola to tea. She liked Lola. Lola was big and fair, and inclined

to plumpness. She had a happy, laughing dispo-
sition and the tea was the jolliest meal that had ever
been eaten at twenty-seven Woodfield Road.
Mabel, with her keen young eyes – and, of course,
common sense – saw at once that Lola was opposite in all ways from her brother, but would be good
for him. Nevertheless, she wondered how on earth
he had met up with her, for Lola talked glibly of
dances and plays and parties. However, she was
glad that at last Lionel was going in for girls.

But Lionel didn't go in for girls, he went in for
Lola, and Lola alone. For the next six months
Lionel spent a sleep-deprived existence. He would
take Lola to a show or a party then have to come
back and work. Sometimes he worked until two or
three in the morning, and Mabel would have to
shake him to get out of bed in time for the office . . .
without breakfast.

Then one night he came in late – early morning
would be more correct – woke her up and told her
that he thought it was awful her having to run the
house on her own, that she really needed someone
to look after her. Practically for no other reason
than this, he had decided to marry Lola.

The door creaked twice during the next three
months, once when Lionel had to go up to London
to take an exam, and again when Mabel pulled it
open to pay the milkman. They still dealt with
Raine's dairy, but now the milk was delivered. It
wasn't the usual milkman this morning, it was Mr
Raine's son. She had seen him two or three times
before. He had started to do the round when the

hired man had his day off. He had looked at the door and said, 'Doesn't that get on your nerves?'

'Oh, it only does it in spasms.'

'Wants a drop of oil, perhaps.' He smiled at her.

She had liked the way he smiled. She had thought, He's nice, and then had said to him, 'We've oiled it all over, and taken it off. Nobody can find where the creak comes from.'

They had both laughed. 'You'll soon be leaving school,' he had said. 'What are you going to do?'

She had looked down and wiped her hands as she admitted, 'I'm not much good at anything. I don't do enough homework. My brother thinks I should take lessons in shorthand and typing . . . Go in an office, you know.'

He had looked round the front garden. 'You won't have much time for homework doing all this, but by, you do keep it nicely. It's not much different from when your parents were alive.' He smiled at her again. 'I remember them. They were mad gardeners, weren't they? You know what I mean?'

Yes, she thought, she knew what he meant, and that was a very good description of them . . . mad gardeners. 'Oh,' she said, 'it isn't like it used to be. It takes too much time, and then there's the house.'

'You do the house?' With each word he nodded.

'Yes.'

'All this place?' He had lifted his eyes up to it.

'Oh, I've got a Hoover and all that,' she answered defensively.

He had looked at her for a long while before

saying, 'You should be out enjoying yourself.'

The milkman was nice.

The week before Lionel and Lola were married, Lola said to Mabel, 'Now, don't expect me to be a mother to you. I don't look the mother type, do I?' They had laughed, and she had ended, 'We'll just be girls together, and you're going to get out and enjoy yourself.'

Another one telling her she was going to enjoy herself. Weren't people nice? It showed that everybody didn't think she was too big, plain and ungainly to go out and have a good time like other girls of her age.

When the couple returned from their honeymoon the house seemed to become a palace of laughter. Lola messed with the cooking, and served up just that, and they all laughed. She attempted the housework, unsuccessfully. And they all laughed. She cut off the bare branches from the mollis azaleas because she thought they were dead, and still they all laughed.

Mabel had never been so happy. She didn't mind coming back from school and doing the washing-up . . . and the cleaning. She didn't mind them going off to a dance or a dinner and leaving her, for they never forgot her, never. She always received something following these dos: flowers that Lola had worn, and the remainder of the chocolates . . . best chocolates. And Lionel never brought a present home for Lola unless he brought her one too. There might be some disparity in the gifts but, then, wasn't Lola his wife? It wasn't the cost of a present but the thought behind it. This was how she looked at it, and everybody was happy.

That was until Lola discovered she was pregnant. It came as rather a shock to her for, as she had clearly stated to Mabel, they had made up their minds not to have any such business for at least five years. She was young and wanted to have some life.

Although, at least in front of her, Lionel acted as if the whole thing had nothing to do with him, Mabel knew he was really very pleased that the natural consequences of marriage had made themselves evident in so short a time. It was years later, when thinking back to the first child, that she had used the idiom 'pulling a fast one'. But at this age, she knew only that her brother was glad he had no longer to keep up the pace of parties, dances and late nights, and could get down to the mountain of work he brought from the office, and which he would have to go on bringing if he wanted the partnership he was after.

The door creaked quite a bit while Lola was carrying the baby, and one night she cried, 'For God's sake! Why can't you put some oil on that thing?'

It was that same night, a week before the summer-holiday break, and for Mabel the end of her schooldays, that Lionel came into the kitchen to talk to her. She was doing her usual last-minute chores – setting the breakfast table for Lionel and herself, and the breakfast tray for Lola. He dropped wearily on to a chair and looked at her. Her busy hands stopped what they were doing when he said,

'You know, I think you're a brick. I don't know what we'd do without you.'

She had never had anyone in her life to throw her arms around, but at this moment she felt such a deep gratitude towards Lionel that she wanted to do just that. Only one didn't do that kind of thing with a brother, and certainly not the Lionel type of brother. For Lionel, despite his parties and dancing, was still a very serious young man, who, in marrying such a girl as Lola, had stepped off the firm earth into the stratosphere, and was even now, after only six months of marriage, finding that his feet were dropping through the vapourish foundation. In fact, it could be said that he had pushed them through, groping for earth again. This had caused his wife to have bouts of morning sickness which she did not like. It could be said that Lionel was a subtly clever young man.

He said, 'You never grumble, never go off at the deep end.' At this stage he wiped his forehead with his fingertips, then added, 'I just don't know how we would carry on without you.'

'Don't be silly.' Once again Mabel felt that the world was a fine place, filled with fine, generous, good people.

He said, 'I was talking to Lola about you going to the typing school. Now' – he put out his finger in the manner of an attorney making a profound statement – 'you're going to that school, don't forget. You're not going to get out of it by what I'm about to say.' And he nodded as she stood before him, the milk jug in her hand. 'It's just temporary . . . until the baby comes. Then things will fall into place. Of course, it will be another few months . . . Well, there it is.'

Like an old judge who had listened to a lot of words and could sum up the issue in question without mistake, she said, 'You mean me to stay at home and look after things? Oh, I'd love that.' She had smiled a big smile of gratitude at her brother, and he had smiled back and heaved a deep sigh, which seemed to relax him.

Lola gave birth to her first baby without a great deal of trouble. It was a girl, and they called her Mary. Mary was a fortnight old when she came home, and every night for three months she did at least two hours' solid yelling . . . and this between two o'clock and four. The doctor said it was nothing more or less than temper, and to let her yell it out. Lola was all for following the doctor's advice and Lola could sleep, but Lionel couldn't. Much less Mabel.

It was about this time that the door started to creak again . . . And the regular milkman became ill. For five weeks, young Mr Raine himself delivered the milk. He always joked about the door. Then one morning he didn't mention the door but, looking at Mabel, said, 'You're looking tired.'

'It's the baby. She's very restless at nights.'

'Do you get up with her?'

'Yes.'

'What's her mother doing?'

'Oh,' Mabel had smiled broadly, 'Lola could

97

sleep through anything – a bombardment or an earthquake.'

'Good for her. And the father?' The milkman did not call him either Mr Campbell or Lionel. When she did not answer he looked at her for a long moment. 'Do you ever go out?'

She did not take this in the form of an invitation – it had not been meant in that way, she knew – but she lifted her chin as she said, 'Yes, yes, of course I go out.'

She felt a slight touch of annoyance, even resentment, that he should ask such a familiar question. But when the door had closed on him, with a creak, she thought, as always, He's nice.

Lola continued to be great fun, and Mabel did not start at the typing school. Lionel made her an offer: She would carry on as usual at home and he would allow her three pounds a week . . . It was marvellous, wonderful. Three pounds a week, able to stay at home and, as Lionel said, be as free as air.

And Lola said there was no reason why they shouldn't start going out and about again: Mabel didn't mind staying in, did she?

Lola was well into her stride of plays and party-going when nature, and Lionel stepping in once more, checked her activities.

Rose was born just one year and nine months after Mary. Exactly eleven months later John came, and thirteen months after this Brian put in his appearance.

Of course, the door went mad at times, creak, creak . . . creak, creak . . . cr-e-ak, cr-e-ak, but there were still periods when it eased up and they didn't hear its voice. That was until the twins arrived. They were a boy and a girl, Tom and Ann. And from the moment they came home the door went berserk.

Lionel had not bargained for twins. He had not really bargained for another baby. Four children, he considered, were an effective barricade against parties and plays. And, what was more, this addition had been sprung on him at a time when they were all, well, pulling in their horns so that he could have a garage built on to the side of the house. Exposed to all weathers, his car was going to rack and ruin.

The twins had reached the crawling stage when, one day, Lionel shook the door, exclaiming through white-heated anger, 'The damn thing!'

And Lola, pulling a long face, remarked to Mabel, 'He should have them all day, shouldn't he?' She was not referring to the creaks but to the twins.

And Mabel, having now reached a point in her life when, for her, the door was always creaking, thought bitterly, So should you. But she never openly quarrelled with Lola. Lola was easy to get on with as long as she wasn't called on to do anything in the nature of housework or the grinding chores attached to young children. She was good at taking the whole tribe of them to the park for a game; she was excellent, between the hours of six and seven, at putting them to bed with laughter and stories, and playful smacks on the buttocks. Lola was such a good playmate that her children declared her tops, while Auntie Mabel at the age of twenty-five had become 'Old Crusty'.

Mary had been born a nasty child, and growing didn't improve her. She was about six when she learnt how to rile Auntie Mabel by moving the door slowly back and forward to a chant: 'Auntie creak . . . Mabel's creak . . . milkman's creak'.

The first time Mabel heard this chant, she wrenched Mary from the door, in no gentle manner, and shook her. Lola had come upon the scene and the first open row had ensued. How dare she shake Mary? Wait till Lionel came in: he would hear something.

When Lionel came in, Lola, still indignant, had ended her report with, 'And all because the child chanted about the milkman.'

'Oh . . . the milkman.' Lionel had turned towards Mabel. 'Don't you think you're letting yourself down chatting so much with that fellow, Mabel?'

'I don't chat with him, I simply pass the time of day . . . or things like that.'

'Things like that!' Lola lifted up her nose. 'You were standing in Leith Road talking to him the other night.'

'How do you know that?'

'I was told.'

'Oh, you were? Well, is there any harm in talking to him? And I only stopped a minute! And you call him the milkman, as if he were dirt. It's his own business.'

'It's his mother's business.' Lionel had nodded slowly at her. 'And will always remain his mother's business. The old girl is as shrewd as ten boxes of monkeys. She's already warned off two applicants for the post of daughter-in-law.'

Mabel found herself burning from the soles of her feet to her cheekbones as she protested, 'Well, I'm not putting in for the post of daughter-in-law. It's coming to something when you can't speak to anyone without being accused of running after them.'

'All right, all right!' Lionel smiled gently at her. 'I'm only pulling your leg. Come on – come on, both of you.' He put his arms around his wife's ample waist and Mabel's bony frame and, squeezing them tightly, he exclaimed, with false jocularity, 'Here am I, a businessman, returned from a heavy day in the office. I want my two handmaidens running around me.'

Before he had managed to end this little play by tickling her ribs, Mabel had pulled herself away from him.

One Saturday morning, Martin Raine called to collect the milk money and, finding Mabel hanging out a large basket of assorted summer wash, he passed her without a word and went to the kitchen door, where the book and the money were already awaiting him. But on his way back he stopped quite close to her and said, under his breath, 'When are you going to kick?' She had a peg in her mouth, and so swiftly had her teeth moved from it that it seemed as if she had spat it out. She stooped to pick it up before looking at him and asking, in a prim tone that did not match her large body, 'What do you mean, when am I going to kick?'

'Do I need to explain? I want to talk to you,' he said.

She had looked startled, not so much at what he had said but because she could see Mary and Rose peeping round the jutting coal-house wall. He had turned his head to follow her glance, then stayed just long enough to look her straight in the eyes and say, 'I'll be outside the museum gates tomorrow around two. I'll hang about for a bit.'

Slowly she turned back to the line and pinned up the last article, a print dress of Mary's.

It was a quarter to three when she reached the museum gates. She did not excuse her lateness, saying, 'I am sorry I've kept you waiting,' for she was so embarrassed she couldn't speak. She had put on flat-heeled shoes to see if this would bring their heads more on a level. Last night she had overheard Lola say to Lionel, 'That milkman, standing jabbering like an old woman. She'll be getting talked about. It's absolute presumption. That individual wants putting in his place. And there's the children . . . Mary notices things.'

Mabel now looked at the little individual. Even with flat heels he was still a shade shorter than herself, perhaps an inch. But he was broad, thickset, and this made him look more of a man than ever Lionel would look with all his weedy six feet. He was quietly dressed, and she thought, He's nicelooking. Everything about him was nice. And this brought an odd pain into her chest.

'Where would you like to go?' he said.

'I'm not . . . I mean I must get back.'

'Why?'

'Because I must, that's all.'

He was standing on the edge of the kerb a few feet away from the museum gate. He said now, 'I'd better put this to you straight. I would like to take you out now and again . . . see more of you. Well?'

She was blushing all over her body. She was twenty-five and no-one yet had asked to see more of her. Boys had always fought shy of her, and Lionel's and Lola's male friends who visited the house didn't see her as someone fit to grace their board, and she knew it. She had the desire to drop her face into the crook of her arm and cry. She said quickly, 'No . . . no, it wouldn't be any use, that's what I've come to tell you . . . I don't want to start anything.' Oh! She almost groaned to herself – that sounded awful . . . she didn't want to start anything!

'Go on, you were saying you didn't want to start anything.'

She moved her head in nervous jerks. 'Well, I thought it better to tell you.'

'Why don't you want to start anything? Is it because your brother is a solicitor and your sister-in-law's on visiting terms with the Whiteheads?'

He was smiling cynically, when she protested, 'No, no! Oh, please! I think you know it isn't that.'

'Well, I hope it isn't.'

'It isn't. But it *is* my brother and his wife, in a way. You see, well, they've come to rely on me so much because of the children.'

'You're twenty-five now, aren't you?' He was sure of her age. 'And you've brought those six children up ... Oh, yes, you have, and from what I've seen, you've done it practically single-handed. Haven't you got wise to them, your brother and her?'

'Oh, please, please!' she protested, strongly now. 'Don't talk of them like that. They've been very good to me, and we've all been happy together.'

'I've no doubt that you've all been happy together.' His voice was quiet. 'And who wouldn't be good to somebody who was shouldering their responsibilities?'

'You mustn't say things like that.'

'They're true nevertheless. The looker-on sees most of the game. And, you know, I'm not only a looker-on, for my mother is a bit of a combination of your brother and his wife.'

He stopped speaking. Her eyes had widened at the mention of his mother, and now he nodded silently at her. 'My life hasn't been exactly a bed of roses. Every time I have attempted to get to know a girl, and I have' – there was that humorous little twist to his lips again – 'my mother has strategically put the damper on it.'

'But wouldn't she do the same . . . well, I mean . . . ?'

'You mean, wouldn't she do the same again? Oh yes, she would, if I let her. Those other times it mustn't have mattered so much. This time it does matter. And I know now it's the only thing that has mattered for years. That's why the other attempts weren't worth the bother of a protest.'

She said, 'Oh, I'm sorry.' And she was sorry. She was more than sorry. There was that acute pain swelling under her ribs, and it could be eased simply by putting out her hand and letting this man take it. But what would Lionel and Lola say? Strangely enough, she was not so afraid of their disdain as of their laughter. Even when she was a young girl and they had laughed at her about the milkman she had felt ashamed, and she knew, with her common sense, that there was no poison so potent as laughter when applied to a young fresh love. Love had to be established before it could stand up to laughter.

He said now, 'There'd be no harm in going for a short walk?'

'No.' She shook her head solemnly. 'It wouldn't be fair.'

'I can stand that kind of unfairness.'

Again she shook her head, and as she said, 'No,' her voice cracked. She put in quickly now, 'I must go. Goodbye.'

'Goodbye.' He did not move, and as she hurried along by the iron railings, which protected the façade of the museum, she almost ran to get away from the desire that told her not to be a fool but to turn and go back to him. This chance might never come again.

When Lionel suggested that it was time she had a holiday on her own, she knew that they had found out about her meeting Martin Raine. Her holidays had generally been spent with the children.

They were troubled, so much so that Lionel told Lola she must tell Mary to tidy up her own room and make her own bed and . . . and dry the dishes.

Mary didn't like this arrangement and she decided to have her own back on Auntie Mabel. She organised a game with which to greet the milkman. It was a crocodile, headed by herself and tailed by Tom. On Saturday morning it dashed from around the coal-house wall and encircled him, chanting gibberish, pointed gibberish. And it went something like:

> Mr Raine
> Waters the milk.
> Mr Raine
> Gives me a pain,
> Auntie Mabel's milkman,
> What a can!

'Auntie Mabel loves the milky-man.' This was Rose's almost hysterically laughing voice.

Mabel could bear no more. She knew that if she went for Mary the crocodile would break up into a scattered, screeching mob, and the whole road would be given over to the milkman's chant. She did the only thing that seemed possible at the moment, she went in and banged the door, which gave a particularly loud creak. As she stood in the scullery with her eyes closed, she heard Mr Raine's voice saying, 'You're a big girl, you're not a baby, and for two pins I'd box your ears for you.'

Then Mary's voice said, 'I'll tell my father what you said when he comes back. You'll get into trouble.'

As good as her word, Mary told her father what the milkman had said to her, and Lionel, although he believed his daughter, asked Mabel for confirmation of this. Yes, Mabel said, it was true. The only thing she regretted was that Mr Raine hadn't boxed Mary's ears.

'It was just as well he refrained,' said Lionel, in a small, cold voice, 'or he might have found himself in court. He might find himself there even yet.'

The outcome of this business was that the Campbells changed their milkman. Their milk was now delivered from the Central Dairies and Martin Raine appeared to drop out of Mabel's world.

Now that there was no more fear of Mabel being whisked off by the milkman, Lola saw no reason to pander to her sister-in-law. The discipline on her daughter was relaxed.

Mary took full advantage of this, and Mabel's large body became so tense that when she dropped wearily into bed at night she thought her bones were riveted together.

Then one Friday morning Martin Raine came into Mabel's life again. She had seen him only twice since Lionel had deprived him of their custom, and both times he had been driving the milk float, but the third time she met him he was dressed as he had been on that Sunday outside the museum gates. He looked excited and happy, like a young fellow of twenty, not a man near forty. He stopped dead in front of her in the square and said, 'Well, hello there.'

'Hello,' she replied.

'Guess what I've just done.' He leant towards her. It was as if they had met only yesterday and had a knowledge of each other's actions.

She smiled at him and shook her head. 'I couldn't.' For a sickening moment she thought, He's got married. But that was silly, he was alone.

He said, 'I've sold the business and I'm going to buy a farm.' He jerked his head towards the high building that housed the solicitor's offices. 'I wouldn't have believed I'd get such a price.'

'Your mother, is she . . . is she pleased about it?'

The smile slid from his face. But not quite: there was still a little quirk round his mouth as he said, 'I don't think she would be if she knew. She died three months ago.'

'Oh, I'm sorry.'

'You needn't be. But we won't go into that. I had a piece of land, you know, to the side of the house, that I used for storage, where the stables were when my father had the horse round. There was a field behind. It was the field they wanted, but I said, "Take all or nothing."' He was smiling broadly again as he said, 'You know what they've given me for the business and that field, two and a half acres of ground altogether? You know what they've given me?'

She shook her head.

'I'm not telling everybody this. I'm not the one to

tell everybody my business, but if I wanted to tell anybody today it would be you. Thirty-two thousand pounds.'

'Thirty-two thousand pounds!' Again she shook her head. Then she smiled, frankly pleased for him. 'I'm glad. Oh, I'm glad. You've worked so hard.'

'Not half as hard as my father did . . . and my mother, give her her due.'

'And you're going to take a farm?'

'Yes – looking on to the moors, you can see for miles and miles. I've had it in mind for a long time, but never thought I'd have the cash.'

They gazed at each other for some moments in silence. 'How are you getting on?' he said.

'All right.'

'Are you happy?'

She paused before answering, 'Yes . . . yes, I'm all right.'

'Just all right?' He was smiling again. 'I want you to see the farm. I think you'd like it.'

When she did not answer he said, 'Have you got time for a cup of coffee?'

She made a sudden decision, and surprised both herself and him when she said, 'Yes . . . yes, I'd like that.'

When they had finished their coffee, he leant his forearms on the table, one on top of the other, and asked, 'May I hope that you'll come out and have a look at the farm?'

She turned her eyes from him. 'I'd . . . better not,' she said.

'What do you think's going to happen when the children grow up and your brother and his wife don't need you any more?'

She looked him straight in the eye as she answered, with dignity, 'I can always work.'

'Yes, that's true. You can always work. Ah, well . . .' It was he who rose to his feet first, and he did not linger over their parting but said, rather briskly, 'Well, goodbye, and thanks for joining me for the coffee.'

'Goodbye.'

She couldn't cry in the bus; she couldn't cry when she reached home; she couldn't cry until late that night when she dropped wearily into bed. And then her heart seemed too tight for the relief of tears. She just lay staring into the darkness, wishing she was the kind of person who could walk out, taking her common sense with her and leaving her subtly selfish brother to cope with his wife and family, and her lazy, indolent, happy-go-lucky sister-in-law to cope with her own children. But she wasn't made that way. She was grateful for the smallest kindness. She couldn't see that Lionel and Lola had been kind to her over the years because of what they got out of her. She couldn't see that they were paying themselves thousands of per cent interest. Until a week later when the door started to creak again, and she actually boxed Mary's ears . . .

John, his knees gripping the paint-scarred surface of the door, one hand on the outer knob while the other clutched the lock, was giving a good impression of a rodeo rider. His yells accompanied the usual creaks from the door. Loud creaks today, shrill, thin creaks.

'Stop that!' Mabel turned from the table, where she had her hands in a basin of flour preparatory to making some pastry for tarts.

The door still swung and creaked, and John still yelled.

'Do you hear me, John? Get off that door at once!'

'Go an' boil your head.'

Mabel flicked her hands downwards to knock the flour from them and rushed to the door, but John, alive to danger signals, had vanished.

Then it was Rose's turn. Creak, creak! . . . Creak, creak!

'Get off that door!'

'Were you speaking to me, Auntie Mabel?'

Then it was Brian.

'Leave that door alone, Brian, will you!'

Once again the game showed evidence of Mary's organisation, and Mabel resisted the temptation to fly to the door and wrench it from the tantalising hands.

As she forced herself to go on with her work a whispered conversation reached her, and when the creak became the accompaniment to the milkman chant, she could stand it no more. She seemed to fly from the table, and so quick was she to reach the door that Mary had no warning. Mabel's hand went out and gripped her niece's shoulder. She shook the surprised girl until her head began to wobble. So startled was Mary that she uttered not a sound. When Mabel ceased, Mary gulped and said, 'You'll – you'll get into trouble for this, you'll see. Wait till my—'

She did not finish what she had to say, for Mabel's hand caught her a stinging slap across the cheek.

The slap brought gasps from the other children, who were staring wide-eyed from safe distances in the yard, but it did not bring Mary to tears. She gave vent to a spasm of furious temper. 'You've hit me! Wait till Mammy comes in. I hate you! And I'll make all the rest hate you. I'll make them drive you round the bend and up the creek . . . creek . . . creek . . . creek. Yes, I will. And I'll tell Mammy I'm not going away with you for our holidays. Stuck in a bungalow for a whole month with you. I'll tell her—'

Mabel moved one step towards Mary and her voice was quiet as she asked, 'What was that you said? What's this about going for a month to a bungalow?'

Mary was still too furious to refrain from repeating what she had overheard her parents discussing, but she backed away as she said, 'When Mammy and Daddy are touring abroad, they're going to make you take us to a bungalow at Dillis Bay, but I'll not go.'

'Ooh! Dillis Bay!' Rose, forgetting the seriousness of the matter, began to hop from one foot to the other. They had all been to Dillis Bay for a week last year, and now she cried, 'Oh, goodie, goodie! I love Dillis Bay. I don't mind going with Auntie Mabel, nor will John, will yo—'

'You shut up!' Mary turned from Mabel to yell at her sister. When she looked back at Mabel she found that her aunt was no longer standing before her but had walked into the kitchen. She called after her, 'You wait until Mammy and Daddy come in.'

Mammy and Daddy came in hot and tired. Mammy had met Daddy after he had left the office and they had gone shopping for clothes for the children. They had done it so often before that it had lost any interest it might once have held. Mammy came into the kitchen first, her eyes looking large in her creamy-skinned face. 'What's this I'm hearing, Mabel? You didn't really slap Mary's face, did you?'

'Yes.' Mabel turned from the stove. 'Yes, I really did, Lola.'

Carefully placing his armful of parcels on a chair and turning slowly towards his sister, Lionel said, 'Do you mean to stand there and tell me, Mabel, that you slapped Mary's face, when you know my views on chastisement?'

'Yes . . . yes, I did.' Mabel was answering this serious accusation in the same light tone she would have used if he had said to her, 'Did you enjoy the pictures?'

Lionel screwed up his eyes. 'Are you all right?' he asked.

Again the answer was positive. 'Yes, I'm all right.' But now Mabel's tone changed and she added, 'I'm all right now, but I think that I've been slightly off my head for years.'

Quick glances were exchanged between Lionel and Lola.

'Oh' – Lola lifted her eyes towards the ceiling – 'now we're going to have hysterics and home truths.'

'No, not hysterics, Lola, home truths, yes. Am I to understand that you've made arrangements for me to take the children, *all of them*, to Dillis Bay for a month, during which time you both will be enjoying a well-earned holiday on the Continent?'

Lionel had the grace to turn away, but Lola said, 'Well, what of it? We've not had a real holiday for years.'

'Nor have I. Only once have I had a holiday. Do you remember, Lionel, when you gave me that ten days in Austria? Well, that's the only holiday I've had without the children since you were married. You've never taken a holiday with the children. How would you like to take them all to Dillis Bay on your own for a month,' Mabel was addressing her sister-in-law, 'and see that they don't choke each other, stab each other, drown each other or, under Mary's dictatorship, jump off the cliff?'

And Lola, hot, tired, and not having a fund of common sense like Mabel, which would have told her at this point to go steady, blurted out, 'That's what you're here for, what you're paid for, to keep them out of mischief.'

'What I'm paid for? Three pounds a week?'

'It isn't only three pounds a week, you've got full board and a nice room.'

'Yes, I've got a nice room when I can get into it.'

'What do you mean?'

'I've been working no less than sixteen hours a day for years, that's what I mean. As for full board . . . Oh, Lola, that's a laugh. People will allow servants to eat off silver platters, these days, so that they can keep them. Don't you know that slaves are hard to come by?'

'Well! Of all the . . . ! How many women would put up with a sister-in-law on top of them all the time, and likely to be? Because I can't see you ever marrying—'

'Lola!' Lionel's voice was almost a bark.

But Lola was hot and tired, and at this moment disturbed at the prospect of the future, but that did not stop her from ending, 'Only the milkman!'

There was a deep silence in the kitchen. Even the children hanging around the open window were silent.

'Lola, you shouldn't have said that.' Lionel was looking angrily at his wife, and now he moved towards his sister and his voice held the old placatory tone when he said, 'Come on, Mabel. What's all this about anyway? Lola's upset. It's very warm out today.'

'Take your hands off me, Lionel.' Mabel turned her head to look at her brother's arm, which encircled her shoulders.

'Oh, come on, don't take it so seriously.'

'Do you think I would marry a milkman, Lionel?'

'No, I don't. I think you've got more common sense. You would never let yourself down that far.'

'Indeed! Well, it just shows how wrong you, of

all people, can be. Because that's what I'm going to do, Lionel. I'm going to marry the milkman.' As Mabel made this statement she felt a tremor of fear streak through her. He had never mentioned marriage, they had never had a chance to get that far. But now she had said it she would have to stick to it.

'Oh, this is the limit.' Lola tore her hat from her head and flung it on to the table. But after this childish action she suddenly became quite still. Her plump body slumped into a chair, and her lips quivered as she looked at Mabel. 'You can't do this. You can't do it.'

'What's to stop me? I am twenty-six, and I have just realised I'm my own boss. Although no-one would ever guess it. And by the way, I had better tell you, I'm not marrying a milkman. Mr Raine is no longer a milkman.' Mabel turned and looked at Lionel. 'He's sold the business, and the land behind the house. It might interest you, Lionel, to know that he received thirty-two thousand pounds for the lot.'

'Thirty-two thou—' Lionel blinked and gaped. 'I don't believe it.'

'No, you wouldn't. And I wouldn't dream of trying to force you. Well, there it is. If you'll excuse me.' She turned with exaggerated politeness to Lola, whose expression now could have made her burst out laughing. 'The lunch is all ready, I'll leave you to it . . . Mary could be trained to dry up for you.' She turned from the quivering Lola and, taking off her apron, said to her stunned-looking brother as she passed him, 'I'll use the phone if I may.'

He did not speak, and there was silence as she went into the hall.

As she lifted the phone her calm front vanished, and her voice was trembling when she gave the number. Perhaps he would be gone. It was a week now since he had told her he had sold the place, he would surely be gone . . . 'Hello, is Mr Raine in, please? . . . Oh, I . . . I didn't recognise your voice.' Her own voice was high as she said, 'It's me, Mabel.'

'Mabel! Oh, Mabel.' In comparison his voice was very low, and the trembling passed from her lips right down to her feet. How was she going to say to him, 'I'm ready if you want me.' She couldn't see his face – he might have changed his mind. Then the next moment she heard herself giving an answer to something he had said to her a long time ago. She said, 'I've done it. I've kicked.'

Silence greeted this statement, and there was fear in her eyes as she took the phone from her ear and looked at it, and then she had to hold on to the little table for support when his deep rumbling laugh came to her. 'When?' he said.

'Just now.'

'What broke the camel's back?'

'Oh, I don't know . . . so many things.' She was whispering. 'But it was that door, you know, the creak in the door that finally did it.'

'When are you leaving?'

'Now.'

'Now!' The voice was loud. 'Do you want me round?'

'Yes, please. Oh, please.' Her voice was so low she had to repeat the statement, 'Yes, please.' She heard his laugh again and his voice saying, 'I'm already there.'

The phone clicked, she turned from the table and pressed her fingers over her mouth, then ran up the stairs to her room.

In five minutes she was down again, a small case in her hand and two coats over her arm. She paused for a moment in the hall, wondering whether she should go into the kitchen, but as she did so Lola's voice came to her, through high hysterical crying: 'You'll just have to do something . . . think of something. You're always so clever at thinking things up. Stop her! You can't let her go.'

Then Lionel's voice, flat, unemotional: 'What can I do? She would go some time. You couldn't expect her to stay here for ever. You'll have to cope, that's all. You'll just have to cope.'

There came a pause in Lola's weeping, and her voice, no longer high, but low, bitter and intense, gave Lionel the biggest shock of the day. 'Cope? You said cope? I've got news for you. I'm going to have another baby!'

Before Lionel had time to come out of his stupor, Mabel made a dash for the front door and ran full tilt down the drive. And if the milkman had not been waiting at the gate, Lionel would surely have caught up with her. But the door of the van was open, his hand was stretched out and, in a matter of seconds, she was being whisked away down Woodfield Road.

Martin didn't stop the van until it was clear of the town. Then he drew up at the side of a quiet road.

When he turned and looked at her she found that she could not meet his eyes. She was trying to steady her trembling hands when he eased them apart gently and took them in his, saying softly, 'Don't shake so, there's nothing to be afraid of. I'm not going to rush you. Anyway, you mightn't want to go through with it when you get a taste of freedom.'

Her head shot up, and her expression was both serious and eager as she said, 'I do. Oh, I do want to go through with it. I've – I've always wanted to go through with it. I must have been a fool, such a fool. If it hadn't been for that creak . . .' The muscles of her face began to twitch. It was even money as to whether she would laugh or cry, and she did both within the next second, for he cupped her face between his two broad hands, looked at her tenderly, and pronounced solemnly, 'God bless that creak.'

As their arms went round each other, and Mabel experienced the first real kiss of her life, every atom that went to make up her large body cried, 'Amen to that.'

6

Lingerie

Miss Robson moved from one high heel – not stiletto, they were not allowed in the department – to the other; then she sighed and muttered something under her breath that sounded very like 'Oh, my God!'

Miss Overton turned her well made-up but ageing face sharply towards Miss Robson. She wanted to exclaim, 'Really, Miss Robson!' but she refrained. In her opinion, Miss Robson was most unsuited to the lingerie department. *This* lingerie department, at any rate. She had been sent from, of all places, the basement – hardware, lino and such. Miss Weir from Personnel had said she couldn't do anything else, with the Christmas rush pending – it was an awful nuisance, Miss Green going sick at this time – and she had apologised.

Miss Weir could apologise to Miss Overton because they had both worked for Watts and Stoddard for twenty years, while Miss Robson had been with the firm for less than twenty months, and was, as Miss Weir had explained, representative of the type that was coming in today.

Miss Robson again moved her position. She was fed up. Fed up to the teeth. Lor', it was bad enough down in Hardware, but you did see people, you had a chance to talk. But here! Three o'clock in the afternoon and they hadn't had a customer since lunchtime, Christmas rush pending or not. They must all be rushing past this department. And no wonder! Who had the money to buy this kind of stuff anyway? The factory managers' wives? Maybe, but although the town was a large industrial one, she couldn't see there being enough factory managers' wives to keep this department going. Look at that bit of nonsense. She stared towards the main stand, which was placed dead centre on the deeply carpeted, screen-secluded corner of the top floor of Watts and Stoddard. There, draped on a piece of contorted Perspex, was a shortie nightdress, so sheer that Miss Robson could see through it to the arched opening that led into the main fashion department. Twenty-four guineas for that! Coo! She could get rigged out top to toe and inside out for less than that. She couldn't see the rush to pay that kind of money for that kind of thing.

Miss Overton was saying, 'You mustn't judge by today, Miss Robson; you've got to take the weather into account. Very often I'm rushed off my feet. What is more, you must realise that this department is for the discriminating shopper, the ladies with accounts.'

'What would you say this one was?'

'What?' Miss Overton turned her head to

follow Miss Robson's wide gaze, and then she was guilty of a slight gape. There, standing within the curved hardwood portals of the partition, was a woman.

Miss Overton kept her eyes fixed on her as she advanced slowly towards the centre display.

'Is she one of your accounts?'

'Don't be vulgar, Miss Robson.' Miss Overton's lips had scarcely parted, and her words were merely a refined murmur. And the murmur went on, 'Watch her! Watch her every move.'

Miss Robson was watching the customer's every move, and with great amusement now; but she kept her voice as low as Miss Overton's as she replied, 'She hasn't got a bag with her.'

'Some of them don't need bags, and these things are so fine they could put them in a handbag or up their sleeves . . . I know. So watch her.'

'You'll be serving her?'

Miss Overton's eyes snapped from the woman, who was still staring at the nightdress, to rest on Miss Robson for a moment. But Miss Robson seemed unaware of their baleful glare. Only that morning she had been pulled up for advancing towards a customer. She had been given to understand, and very firmly, that Miss Overton must always make the first move, at least when there was only one customer. But Miss Overton was making no move towards this customer: she just stood staring until the woman turned and came towards the small glass counter.

It would have been hard to gauge her age. She

could have been anything between fifty and seventy. Her face had a grey look and was etched with fine wrinkles. What could be seen of her hair under the shapeless felt hat was also grey. In fact, you could say she was grey all over, a dirty grey. Her coat, which was buttoned high up to the neck, had the appearance of having been slept in. But the parts of her that interested Miss Robson most were the woman's legs and feet. The legs, thin, almost like straight sticks, were covered with a pair of concertinaed grey lisle stockings, one hanging so loosely it suggested that it was held up only by a slack garter. The shoes, too, were grey, flat-heeled and worn, and Miss Robson noted, with a gathering of her brows, that the woman's feet were wringing wet.

'Good afternoon.'

The voice brought Miss Robson's eyes from the floor to the woman's face. The voice, so in contrast with the woman's appearance, surprised not only Miss Robson but also Miss Overton, so much so that she forced herself to answer as if she were dealing with a customer . . . a valued customer: 'Good afternoon, madam.'

'You have some beautiful things.' The grey face turned slowly and looked from the nylon briefs to the bras, the slips, the nightdresses, the pyjamas, the corselettes, for which the only word was enchanting, then back again to Miss Overton, and she said, 'May I see some, please?'

Miss Overton swallowed. She moved her hands

along the glass counter as if she were stroking silk. She resisted turning to look at Miss Robson, and then said, 'What have you in mind, madam?'

'Oh.' The eyes flicked again from one article to another. 'I think I'll start with the cami—brassières,' she said.

Miss Robson was gaping now. The woman had been going to say camisoles. Her granny still called bras camisoles, but this woman wasn't nearly as old as her granny.

Miss Overton said, 'Certainly, madam.' But instead of going to the glass drawer where the bras were kept, she went behind Miss Robson and, in passing, gave her a slight dig. Miss Robson turned and watched her very superior superior going into the changing room. She was in there only a few minutes before she returned, and again gave Miss Robson a covert dig in the back.

Miss Robson was quick on the uptake – she came from a part of the town where this instinct was part of survival – and she now went towards the changing room. There, from a chair, she picked up the note Miss Overton had written. It said simply, 'Get Miss Slater.'

Miss Slater, splay-footed Slater, the store detective. But the old woman hadn't done anything yet. Well, she supposed old Enamel Face knew what she was about.

She walked sedately out of the changing room, across the thick carpet, and on to the main floor. There, as on all floors, was a departmental telephone. She rang the central office and asked them to pass on Miss Overton's message. Then she returned to the lingerie department.

The customer was now saying, 'Yes, I think I'll have that, it's so pretty.'

Miss Robson, looking at Miss Overton, saw that she was in a stew. And no wonder, she thought, if the old dear was going in for five-guinea slips.

As she took her place behind the counter again, the woman pointed upwards and asked, in that surprising voice, 'What are those?'

Miss Robson wanted to let out a high laugh: the old girl was pointing to the falsies.

Miss Overton coughed and tried to keep her eyes on a level with the customer's face and not let them slip down to the board-flat chest. 'They are, madam . . . they are to go inside the brassière.'

'Oh!' The woman moved her head slowly as if discovering a surprising truth, and then she said softly, 'Really? Perhaps I could try them when I . . . when I try the corselette. I would like that one, I think.' The customer was now pointing to a work of art in nylon, silk and lace.

Miss Overton allowed herself the relief of a gulp. Her mind was in a disturbing whirl. What was she going to do? One had to be so careful. But she couldn't allow this – this drab creature to try on the exquisite creation. If only Miss Slater would come through. Miss Weir always said, you never could tell. But even she would be able to tell by looking at this person. And yet, when she spoke . . . If only Miss Slater would put in an appearance!

Miss Overton looked down at the selected garments lying on the glass counter to her right hand, and she said quietly, 'You have chosen three slips, three pairs of panties, three brassières. You would like to see the corselette, madam? I'm afraid it's rather expensive. It is fifteen guineas, madam.'

'Oh, that's all right. I'm going to buy a hundred pounds' worth.'

Now she had heard everything, and Miss Robson bit hard on her lips to stop herself bursting out laughing. When she looked at Miss Overton, that prim lady had so forgotten herself that, under cover of the counter, she was spreading out her hands in a hopeless appealing gesture. And because the customer had now turned from her and was looking towards the central display stand, Miss Overton went further. Glancing at Miss Robson, she quickly tapped her forehead.

This action coming from Miss Overton was on a level with an exchange of confidences, and Miss Robson allowed her grin to widen.

As they both stood side by side now, watching the customer walking slowly round the stand holding the nightdress, Miss Overton murmured something that Miss Robson didn't catch, so she said, 'Pardon?'

'*Non compos mentis.*'

'Pardon?' Miss Robson's smile had faded.

'She's *non compos mentis.*'

Compos mentis? What did she mean by that? Showing off her education. She likely meant the old girl was bats.

'I will take that nightdress as well.'

Miss Overton was lost for words, when Miss Slater came through the archway.

Miss Slater did not look like a store detective. She was not the thin snipy type, she was inclined to roundness, with a face that looked ordinary. She was a woman who would pass in a crowd, which was why she was a good store detective.

Because she received no signal from either of the assistants, she began to behave as a customer and view the display. And as she acted the part, Miss Overton's voice, slightly louder than usual, came to her saying, 'The articles you have chosen, madam, come to about sixty pounds. Is that all right?'

'Yes. I told you, I'm going to buy a hundred pounds' worth.'

Miss Slater took up a position where she could have a better view of the customer, and she decided immediately that things were fishy, to say the least. Yet she knew she had to be careful.

'May I sit down?' The customer was holding on to the glass counter; her voice had changed, her words coming slowly now.

'Certainly, madam. Certainly.' It was Miss Overton who spoke, but it was Miss Robson who went round the counter and pushed a chair forward for the customer. She watched the woman sit down slowly; she watched the greyness of her face turn to a pasty white; and she bent over her as she said, 'May I . . . may I have a glass of water?'

Miss Robson looked at Miss Overton, and Miss

Overton said, 'Get the lady a glass of water, Miss Robson, please.'

But before Miss Robson had time even to turn away, she found her hands shooting out involuntarily towards the woman as she slid sideways from the chair.

In a second Miss Overton was round the counter, and Miss Slater, moving briskly across the carpet, said, 'She's fainted,' then, 'Better get her out of this.'

'Where?'

'The changing room. We can't have her lying here in case anyone comes in. And go and get that water.' This command was directed to Miss Robson.

Without difficulty the two women carried the inert figure of the customer into the cubicle, and laid her out on the floor. They stood one on each side looking down on her. Then Miss Slater repeated Miss Overton's previous remark, but in plainer language: 'Mental, I should say.'

'Yes, decidedly. Sixty pounds' worth she's chosen. She said she wanted to buy a hundred pounds' worth.'

'No doubt. Don't we all?'

At this point Miss Robson entered the cubicle with a glass of water, and Miss Slater, taking it from her, knelt down by the woman. But although she moistened her lips and sprinkled some on her forehead, now minus the hat, the customer did not immediately respond.

'This is dreadful. What are we going to do?' Miss

Overton was clasping her hands first one way, then another, and she looked at Miss Slater who was obviously thinking deeply. Then Miss Slater spoke. 'Dr Bygate is down in the basement doing his weekly check,' she said. 'I think I'd better call him.'

'Yes. Oh, yes.'

Ten minutes later Dr Bygate entered the cubicle. The customer was still on the floor, but propped up against the partition now, and her weary eyelids lifted at the sound of a man's voice exclaiming, 'Miss Atkinson!'

'Oh, you . . . you, Doctor?'

'Why, Miss Atkinson, fancy running into you here. What is the matter? You're not feeling too well?'

'I must have fainted. How nice to see you, Doctor.'

'It's nice to see you, Miss Atkinson.' The doctor had hold of the woman's wrist now, and after a few moments, he said, 'When did you last have a meal, Miss Atkinson?'

'Oh, I'm not quite sure, Doctor. Eating doesn't matter any more.'

'Oh, you mustn't think like that, Miss Atkinson. But tell me, where are you living? You went off so suddenly . . . But there now . . . there now.'

Miss Atkinson was crying quietly, the tears rolling slowly down her flat white face. She said, 'I'm sorry, Doctor. I'm sorry to give way.'

'Nonsense!' The doctor's voice was brusque. 'You give way all you like, cry your fill.'

'You were always kind, Doctor. I suppose . . . I suppose you were surprised to find me here, in this kind of shop, at least this department.'

The doctor turned and looked at Miss Overton before replying, 'Not at all, not at all. Why shouldn't you be in this department?'

'Why shouldn't I, Doctor? I've always asked myself that question, why shouldn't I? I love pretty things.' Miss Atkinson's head drooped forward and fell on to her chest, and she murmured, 'She was cruel, Doctor, so cruel.'

When he said, 'Come along and sit on this chair,' Miss Slater and Miss Overton lifted Miss Atkinson as though she were a feather on to it, and apparently to the man's satisfaction, for he said quietly, 'She'll be all right, just leave her.'

Miss Overton and Miss Slater passed round the cubicle's curtain and joined Miss Robson on the other side. And now they moved a little distance away, but not so far that they couldn't hear what was being said on the other side of the silk drapery.

The doctor was saying, 'Old people do unaccountable things, Miss Atkinson.'

'But she knew what she was doing, Doctor. It was so cruel. You know, Doctor, I went there when I was twenty-two. She wasn't fifty then, and I stayed, not because I liked her . . . perhaps you don't know this, Doctor, but I loved Gerald. That's why I stayed. I used to believe what he said, that we'd be married one day after she was gone. She wouldn't have left him a penny if he had taken me, I knew that, so I was quite willing to wait. I waited thirty-three years, Doctor. But he married that Italian woman. And his mother was so furious she cut off his allowance and eventually she made a new will: I was to have the house and enough to live on. She said to me, "Could you live on a thousand a year, Gwendoline?"' The cubicle resounded to sad, weird laughter. 'It was at a time when she thought I was going to leave her that she said that. And she had the solicitor come to the house and everything was settled. Old Mr Haig was the solicitor. You knew him, Doctor, he was a nice man, and he said, "You've worked for this, Miss Atkinson, if anyone has." But Mr Haig died, as you know, and it must have been some time when I was out that she sent for his partner – oh Doctor, how could she? – to leave everything to Gerald. Not one penny after thirty-three years! She said in the will that I was left to Gerald's generosity. Oh, she was cruel: she knew what Gerald's generosity was like better than anyone. Even before she cut him off he hardly visited her more than once a year, and then only to make sure that his allowance would continue. She was a cruel woman.'

'Don't fret, Miss Atkinson. Don't worry.' He had hold of her hand now. Yes, she certainly had been a cruel woman. He had never cared much for Mrs Windom. But she had been a patient of his for years and he had made her end easy, though at this moment he found himself hoping she was getting her just deserts. Cruel? That wasn't the name for it. Sadistic evil was more like it. He had known Miss

Atkinson for the last twenty years. He could remember her mainly as a flitting grey shadow going between the front door and Mrs Windom's room. He had once thought of her as a pretty dried-up flower that had kept its scent. The scent, in her case, was her voice. He said now, 'But where did you go? You shouldn't have gone off without letting me know. You know I would have helped you.'

'Yes, Doctor, yes. You were always kind, so kind. Sometimes I used to cry because you were kind. But I couldn't bear any more. When I knew that everything was to go to Gerald – she hadn't even left me the furniture in my room – I couldn't stand it, Doctor, I couldn't. Gerald didn't come until the day of the funeral and then he hardly looked at me. Mr Walters, who read the will, said he would do what he could for me. He seemed very sorry and was kind. He said I was to call at the office in a week's time. I've called every week for the last three months, and yesterday I received Gerald's generosity.' She was staring up at the doctor, her eyes blurred with the pain and humiliation of years of servitude. 'He had sent me a hundred pounds. A hundred pounds, Doctor! His mother had left seventy-four thousand and he had sent me a hundred pounds.'

In the lingerie department at the end of the glass counter, Miss Overton and Miss Robson exchanged glances. Then they looked at Miss Slater. As if controlled by the same thought their heads moved simultaneously from side to side. Then Miss

Slater turned away and went hurriedly through the curved archway.

'Don't cry any more, Miss Atkinson. There now, there now, it's all over.'

'It's done me good to cry, Doctor, as you said. You see, I haven't been able to cry. Do you know what she bought me every year for a Christmas box, and for my birthday, Doctor?'

'No, Miss Atkinson.'

'Well, Doctor, for Christmas she bought me a winceyette nightdress, and for my birthday, which falls in June, she bought me a Celanese slip. Every year, Doctor, it never changed. And yesterday, when I got Gerald's bounty, I had a strange idea. It seems silly now, quite silly, knowing how little I have to live on, and a hundred pounds is a hundred pounds, but I felt I must spend it all on nice underwear. Can you understand that?'

'Yes, Miss Atkinson, I can understand it very well indeed.'

'I'm so glad, Doctor. You see, look, I've the hundred pounds in my bag. I cashed the cheque this morning, and I couldn't get the idea out of my head that the only thing I wanted in life was some beautiful underwear, a beautiful slip or a nightie. Perhaps, Doctor, it was because when I was young I longed for beautiful, flimsy things. So silly. What am I going to do now? I was going to buy these things – they're lovely, exquisite – but I'll never be able to wear them, will I?'

'Don't worry, Miss Atkinson. Don't worry your head about a thing. Now, look' – he bent over her and glanced at his watch as he did so – 'in half an hour I have an appointment, but there's plenty of time for me to run you home . . . not to your home, to mine.'

'Oh, but—'

'Now don't say a word. My wife will be delighted to see you; in fact I can speak for her and say that she will be delighted to have your company for a few days . . . say, over Christmas?'

'Oh, no! No!' Miss Atkinson was sitting up now protesting with her hands and voice.

'You'll do as I say, Miss Atkinson. And I can assure you you'll be very welcome. Now, no more.'

Whilst he had been speaking, the doctor had wondered if he would have time to phone his wife and prepare her. But no, he thrust the idea aside. In a case like this surprise was the better tactic. And anyway, lately Evelyn had been going in for good works. Well, here was a good work, definitely worthy of her attention, one she could get her teeth into.

As he helped the thin, grey Miss Atkinson to her feet, his mind was racing ahead. He had only another year before he retired, and he wasn't without some say in this town, and if it was the last thing he did he would see that this poor creature from a dying generation, perhaps the last of that generation of refined slaves, would end her days in comfort. The council was benevolently putting up very nice flats for the old people of the town. The tenants would be a selected group. Well, he would see that Miss Atkinson was one of them.

When the doctor lifted the curtain aside and assisted Miss Atkinson through into the department, there was only Miss Overton awaiting them. Miss Robson was at the counter, feverishly sorting the underwear on the glass shelf. It was this activity that dragged Miss Overton's gaze from the customer and the doctor towards her assistant.

When she realised what Miss Robson was about to do she took a number of quick, prim steps to the front of the counter and whispered, 'What are you doing, Miss Robson?'

'I'll pay for it, don't worry. It's this.' Quickly Miss Robson jerked a pale rose nylon slip on to a clear part of the glass, and, folding it swiftly, she thrust it into one of the fancy containers the store provided for their luxury articles.

The doctor and Miss Atkinson were passing the centre display when Miss Robson called, 'Just a minute.'

It was no way to address Dr Bygate, yet Miss Overton had no reprimand for her assistant. But when Miss Robson came round the counter and made to move towards the doctor and Miss Atkinson, Miss Overton's hand checked her. She did not put her hand on Miss Robson's arm but laid it gently on top of the bag, which Miss Robson was holding with her two hands. Looking straight at Miss Robson, she said, under her breath, 'It can be from us both.'

Miss Robson's mouth dropped open until she hastily closed it.

Well! Who would have thought it? Then she said under her breath, 'OK,' and they both moved forward to the customer.

It was the customer who spoke first: she said, 'I'm sorry, so terribly sorry, for . . . for all this inconvenience . . .'

'Here.' Miss Robson thrust the package towards Miss Atkinson. 'A Christmas box for you.'

'From us both.' Miss Overton was smiling gently and her voice was no longer prim.

'But . . . but . . .' Miss Atkinson looked at the doctor. She looked at Miss Overton, and then she looked at Miss Robson – Miss Robson, who was young and pretty. She shook her head and said, 'Oh! my dears, my dears.' And then the tears spurted from her eyes and choked her words. 'I-c-can't.'

'Yes, you can.' It was Dr Bygate now, lifting her hand to take the gift.

Miss Atkinson looked down at the gaily coloured bag – at least, she turned her flooded eyes in its direction.

Miss Overton was aware of a constriction in her throat, she would never have termed it a lump, and she did not shudder, nor did any reprimand rise to her lips when she heard Miss Robson, in anything but a high-class department-store tone, say, 'Look, I'll get yer address from the doctor and come and see you an' fetch you round to me granny's. She's a great girl, is me granny.'

'Oh, my dears.' Although the repeated phrase now sounded pathetic and sad, it also conveyed an expression of joy. Miss Atkinson looked from Miss Robson to Miss Overton: Miss Overton wasn't beautiful, and Miss Atkinson seemed to catch at something in her that was akin to something in herself, and she said again, her words now slow with feeling, 'My dears. My dears.'

Miss Robson and Miss Overton stood side by side watching the customer leave the department on the arm of Dr Bygate. It seemed as if she was less grey, less stooped now. Although her stockings were still corkscrewed about her legs, and the creases in her coat were more evident, they did not make for greyness. After a moment Miss Overton turned abruptly, went to the counter and began in a busy fashion to sort out the lingerie. It was quite some time before she spoke. Eventually she said, 'It was five guineas but we will get a discount.'

Miss Robson too went around the counter, and now she was standing facing Miss Overton. She looked at her superior and made a surprising remark: 'You're all right,' she said.

'Well,' said Miss Overton, keeping her eyes purposely from Miss Robson's, and speaking as if the idea of the gift had been entirely her own, 'as I always say, "There but for the grace of God . . ."'

'That's funny, that's what me granny's always saying, "There but for the grace of God goes me."' Then Miss Robson added quite an irrelevant remark. She said, 'I like being up here. If there's a permanent going anytime I wouldn't mind asking Miss Weir for it.'

And, after a slight pause, Miss Overton, her hands moving slowly now, said, 'I'll see what I can do.'

7

'Nasty! Don't Touch!'

'Nasty! Don't touch.' It was a phrase Louise Harding had been apt to use more than was necessary, even when her daughter Lorna was well past childhood. She had used it as a warning, and with equal emphasis against worms, children with dirty noses and dogs. And now Lorna was applying the same sentiment to her mother and the man who was standing by her side, the man she herself was to marry in four weeks' time.

Her amazed gaze had settled on her mother's face. She had always known that her mother was pretty; she hadn't always known that she was also petty, vain and selfish. She had discovered these latter qualities about four years ago when her father, who had been ailing for some time, decided wisely to take a less responsible post. His decision had met with furious opposition from her mother: a holiday she would allow, for he was tired, but to demote himself! Had he thought what it would mean to lose the car, the gardener, the oiled routine of the house?

David Harding had taken a holiday, which had

enabled him to carry on for two further years. He had died a year ago, not quickly but painfully. It had been very distressing to Louise Harding, she told all her friends. Lorna had tried to forget that her mother was responsible for her father's death; and she had tried to comfort her, as had Charles. Charles had been wonderful with her mother, and she had thought at the time how lucky she was to have him. Charles had seen to everything. An accountant, he knew about money, and this was fortunate because her mother was concerned about how she was going to manage, even survive. But Charles had reassured her. 'Don't worry, Mammy Lou,' he had said, 'just leave everything to me.'

Mammy Lou was Charles's pet name for her mother. She didn't like it very much: she said it made her feel ancient. But Charles had assured her that she would remain a girl until she died.

Her mother liked Charles; she said he was such a comfort.

Three months after David Harding's death Charles had suggested that he and Lorna should be married quietly and live with her mother.

Up to now, because Charles was so wise – he was ten years older than herself – she had agreed with almost every suggestion he made, but that she should start her married life in the house where she had lived for twenty-five years created in her an obstinacy that surprised her, and Charles even more. He could not understand her attitude: it was a beautiful house; it would be years before they could furnish a place anything like it. He did not voice the latter thought but Lorna sensed what was in his mind, and she could not explain to him that the idea of starting her married life in this house repelled her.

Oddly enough, her mother, too, had opposed Charles's wishes. Apparently, she was also against a quiet wedding: they must wait a little longer and do the thing properly.

It was decided to 'do the thing properly' in March, although Lorna considered March a beastly month. She even said as much to Charles but, as Charles laughingly replied, what was the weather compared to a saving on tax?

Her mother's voice now pierced the pain in her mind: 'Don't look at me like that, Lorna. I haven't committed a crime, no matter what you might think.'

Lorna shook her head slowly and continued to look at her mother. She could not speak, she could not string words together to express the feeling of nausea that was swirling through her body. As she stared at her mother's face, she was not seeing it as it appeared now, but as she had seen it looking over Charles's shoulder from within the circle of his arms. And she felt that until her dying day she would not be able to erase the picture from her mind.

She had left the house only an hour earlier to spend the night with Faye. Faye had been her friend since schooldays and was to be chief bridesmaid. They were to go through some pattern books and decide on the dresses. But when she had reached Faye's, it was to find the house in an uproar, with her friend's twin schoolboy brothers in bed with mumps. Faye's mother had said, in her forthright north-country manner, 'Go on, you, Lorna, get yourself away home. I don't want them to shoot me if the wedding's postponed.'

So Lorna had returned home. She had let herself in through the back door. Her habit of changing her shoes outside in the porch might have been why neither her mother nor Charles had heard her entering. But they should have heard the kitchen door opening. Perhaps the sound of the television covered it. Across the well-carpeted hall the drawing room almost faced the kitchen, and it was in the mirror above the fireplace that she saw, entwined, the arms of two people. It was a wonder also that they didn't hear her breath catch in her throat, for it seemed to block her breathing. The effect was excruciating, so much so that she made a sound like a groan.

She was standing in the drawing-room doorway, transfixed, as her mother's lips parted from Charles's and her head rested on his shoulder.

Louise Harding was saying now, 'These things happen. We couldn't help ourselves.'

Lorna's head was still moving from side to side.

'I'm still young,' Louise Harding cried at her daughter. 'You seem to forget that. I've my life before me, I deserve happiness as much as you do . . . And there's less difference between my age and Charles's than yours and his. Don't stand there looking like that – it isn't the end of the world.'

It was at this point that Charles moved towards Lorna. As he stepped forward his hand came out and almost touched her. But as if she were warding off the searing pain of a branding iron, she jumped away from it.

'Don't ever touch me again, do you hear? Never! Never!' The voice was strange and hard, not like her own. She was firing words at him now and he lowered his head against their impact: 'This didn't start today or yesterday, it's been going on for weeks. Weeks, hasn't it? You! Such a paragon of all the virtues. Remember what you said about your sister Jessie, because she had to get married – remember? That the family was right to turn her adrift! There was too much latitude allowed people today. You said that – too much latitude.' She was laughing now, a high, terrifying sound, and as it went on she heard her mother shout above it, '*You* are just like your father, deep, crafty. If you knew it was going on, why didn't you say something?'

Lorna's head went back, and again that weird laughter was rising in her. Her mind was repeating, 'Crafty . . . say something.' It was funny, very funny.

With a startling suddenness that was as frightening as the laughter, there settled on her a quietness. She looked from Charles to her mother and back to Charles. Then she said, 'I hope you enjoy each other.'

As she left the room, Charles's voice followed her: 'Wait, Lorna. Wait!' But he didn't come into the hall: her mother saw to that.

The quietness was still in her as she packed a small case.

As she came down the stairs her mother was waiting: there was not a vestige of remorse on her face. She looked at her daughter and said, 'I shall send the remainder of your things to Faye's. I'm going to Harrogate for the next few weeks.' Then, as Lorna passed her, she spoke to her back. 'I'm not sorry about this. You could never really love Charles as I do. You are too like your father, too hard to be capable of any real feeling. I'm not going to worry about you. You'll get by.'

As Lorna left the house and walked into the dark drizzle, the calm feeling remained with her, and as she walked along the tree-shaded terrace where the élite of Eastshields lived, she thought that this feeling must be similar to the calm that had kept her father from murdering his wife.

Eastshields was a town of sharp contrasts. You emerged abruptly from the Layton quarter on to the main road. On the other side was what was known as the Old Dock. This quarter took up more than half of the town. As the name implied it housed the docks, also the factories, the market and a warren of little streets, along which the wind from the North Sea seemed perpetually to blow.

During the whole of her life she hadn't been down to the Old Dock more than half a dozen times and then with her father when he took her to see the ships. So why had she crossed the road and walked into the Old Dock quarter now?

Her step quickened as she passed the ferry landing and turned off along by the wall of the dock. The quiet feeling was still with her but it had changed. It no longer seemed part of her, it had become something outside herself. She imagined that her father was walking beside her and it was the quietness that had been in him that was speaking to her now. Once she stopped, put the case on the greasy pavement and stood listening to the voice. And as she listened she began to cry, painful, hard sobs; crying that burned her throat, and swelled her lungs until they seemed to be forcing her ribs apart. Her father's voice was saying to her, 'Don't cry, my dear, don't cry. Nothing in life is worth crying over. I found that out. Life is so futile.'

She picked up her case and walked on, her head down almost on her chest. Two young fellows, coming towards her, parted to let her pass, and nudged her with their elbows. When she paid no attention to them they turned and peered after her through the murky light.

She had reached the dock gates now but she knew she couldn't go through them because of the man on duty there. However, she dimly remembered a wall further along to the left where the children used to sit. Her father had hoisted her up on to it once so that she could see the ships moored against the jetties.

When she reached the place where the wall

should have been it was to find an open space. A street-lamp showed her a patch of wasteland and in the far distance the glint of lights bobbing in the river. She did not see the inert bulldozers and cement mixers of the building site that the area had become, she saw nothing but the lights guiding her to the water.

Just before she stepped from the roadway on to the rubble a man passed her. His head was down against the wet wind and he was holding on to his cap. He, too, was carrying a case. He paused for a moment and called after her, 'Here! Here, miss! Where you going?'

His voice startled her, and she began to run in and out of the obstacles that were preventing her direct approach to the river. As she rounded a crane she flung away her case. Why was she carrying that? She had lost the glint of the lights in the water, and as she turned to look back she saw against the lesser darkness the figure of the man behind her. He was within the enclosure now and standing quite still. Then he seemed to spring into the air as he came after her.

She was running wildly now and terrible moans were grinding through her body.

One moment she saw the oil on the water with the lights chopping it into pieces, then the reflection was jammed from her sight and the man was holding her by the shoulders. As she struggled with him a voice called through the darkness, 'What's goin' on there?' The man put his arms around her and pressed her face into his coat. Her mouth was hard against his wet mackintosh, and as she strained to draw breath, she heard him answer, 'Nothing. It's all right, we came in the wrong gate,' before he hissed at her, 'Ssh! Be quiet! It's the dock polis.'

'What are you doing here?' It was the voice coming nearer.

'I tell you we came in the wrong gate, we're goin' – come on!' As the light picked them up he put his arm around her shoulders and hurried her away, further into the darkness.

He did not speak until they emerged on the road again, where there was no light. He was still holding her and he said, 'Don't cry.' His voice was soft and thick with a north-country burr.

'Le-let me go.'

'I'm doing no such thing. You know what will happen to you if you attempt to take to the water. That place is alive with little boats. They'll pull you out and you'll be in court the morrer mornin'. Don't you realise that?'

'Let me go!'

'Not on your life. And, look, I'm in a hurry . . . Come along with me.'

'No! No, I'm not going. Let me go! I'll scream.'

'Well, that's up to you. You scream and you'll have that dock polis here like a flash of lightning. I'm tellin' you.'

'I'm going home.'

'I don't believe you. And, look, as I said, I'm in a hurry. I have ten minutes at the most. You've got to come along.'

'Where do you want to take me?'

'I'm going to take you home – to my home.'

'I don't believe you. I don't want to go. Why should you?'

'Look, I've told you and I can't stop here arguing. You either come with me now or I'll do the calling for the polis. It's one or the other. I'm not leaving you here alone . . . And get it into your head, I'm not tryin' to abduct you or any such nonsense as that. You're bad . . . ill, you need attention, at least somebody with you.'

'I don't need anyone with me. I just want you to leave me alone.'

He stood back from her a moment. She couldn't see his face, only the huge bulk of him. He wasn't much taller than her but he seemed to be of great breadth and strength, and his next words bore this out when he said softly, 'You know, I've only to give you a crack on the jaw and you'd be out.' Then, his voice dropping to a soft whisper, he went on, 'If I was to bring someone to you, a woman, would you go with her?'

'But why should you?'

'Look, there's no time to go into the reasons why anyone does anything, I've got to get crackin'. Here . . .' When she heard him tear open his mac, she pressed herself against the blank factory wall, and when his hand sought hers she only just stifled a high scream. As he pressed something into her palm, he said rapidly, 'I'm leaving this with you. In this little box is something I value very much. I'm not religious or anything like that but I've carried it with me for years. Somebody gave it to me when I was a lad. If I lost everything else in the world I wouldn't want to lose that, so I'm trusting you with it. Look, promise me on it that you'll stay put till somebody comes for you . . . Go on.' When she did not answer he said rapidly, 'I'm trusting you, mind. Time's running out and I've got to pick up my case. You could save me all this rush if you'd only come along. Will you?'

Still she made no answer, and the man said, 'Good enough.' He backed two steps from her, then turned and disappeared like vapour into the darkness.

Lorna's fingers groped round the little shape in the palm of her hand. She hadn't promised anything. Whatever it was she could leave it on the pavement. She slumped now against the wall. She would go and find her case. She would not go near the water again, that was past, but she must get away from here.

But she did not move from the wall. She had the sensation that her body was sinking into the stone, and all of a sudden she felt sick. It was as if she had been in the river and swallowed a stomach full of dirty water. She turned sideways and leant her cheek against the rough bricks, and when she retched for the second time, a firm hand was placed on her brow and a woman's voice said, 'That's it, get it up. Get it up, lass, you'll feel better.' After some minutes had passed the woman said again, 'Come along, it's only two streets away.'

'My – my case.' Lorna pointed a wavering finger in the darkness.

'Whereabouts?'

'Somewhere in there.'

'Don't worry. I'll send one of the bairns with a light. They'll pick it up. Come along now.' The woman put her thick arm around Lorna's back, with the hand under her armpit, and Lorna had the sensation that she was being carried through the darkness . . .

'In you go.'

The room into which she stepped from the street had no light of its own, but in a reflection from a doorway at the far end she had the impression of a huddle of furniture, in the middle of which stood a bed; and then she was in the other room, blinking in strong light that seemed to be reflected back from every corner, from the glass in the many pictures hanging on the walls, the horse brasses hanging around the fireplace, the polished mahogany table, and the numerous straight-backed chairs. It was reflected from the spectacles in the hand of an old man who was sitting in a basket chair to the side of the fire. When he smiled at her and said, 'Hello, lass,' she could not answer. She turned from his gaze and looked at the woman, seeing her for the first time. She might have been sixty or more but she looked strong and broad like the man in the darkness.

Now, the woman was standing behind her, her hands on her shoulders, and she was saying, 'Get your coat off you, it's wringing wet. What you want is a strong cup of tea and something to eat.' Then, without a pause, she went on, 'This is me husband. You mustn't mind him not gettin' to his feet, but he hasn't been on them for the last fifteen years.'

Lorna looked at the woman, and from her to the man. Their faces looked remarkably alike as if they were brother and sister, and they were both smiling kindly at her. With a swift movement, she turned from them, sat down and dropped her head on to her arms on the table. And when the sobs shook her and her crying filled the room, they did not come near her: the man sat looking at her and the woman went into the scullery to brew the tea.

The next morning Lorna awoke in the smallest room she had ever seen. Without exaggeration she knew that if she spread her arms wide, her fingers could almost touch each wall. The room held nothing but the single bed, a wardrobe in the corner, and a little table, beside which stood her case. She knew that the name of the people who lived in this house was Butting, and that the man who had saved her from the river was Mrs Butting's lad, as she called him – and he a second engineer on a tanker – and he had been on his way to the main dock to join his ship when he had met her.

When Mrs Butting brought Lorna her breakfast on a tray covered with a hand-crocheted cloth, she said, 'Now, what you've got to do is stay put in that bed for a couple of days until you pull yourself together. If you want to tell me anything, you can, and if you don't it's all right with me. But what you've got to do is to sort yourself out.'

Lorna started to cry again, and she touched Mrs Butting's hand. 'You're so kind.'

'Kind nowt,' replied Mrs Butting. 'If we can't do a turn for a body, what are we here for?'

On the second day Lorna wrote Faye a letter, and on the third day Faye came to number fifteen Pilot Street.

As she sat on the side of the bed in the little room and looked at Lorna, she exclaimed, in almost horrified tones, 'How on earth did you land here? Why didn't you come to us?'

Ignoring this, Lorna asked, 'What's happened?'

Faye shook her head. 'Your mother thinks you're with us, she sent all your things along. I went to see her this morning but there was no answer. The house looks shut up.'

'Do you know if anything's happened to the flat?' Lorna asked.

Faye's eyes dropped away from hers and she said, 'I understand from Neil Parkinson that Charles asked one of the men in the office if he would like to take on the lease.' Now Faye reached out impulsively and caught at Lorna's hands. 'Oh, Lorna, it's dreadful, terrible. Who would have thought of such a thing? Charles of all people. He was so – so—'

'Don't talk, Faye. Please don't talk. It's finished.'

'Are you coming back with me now?'

'No . . . I'm staying here.'

'What? Here?' Her friend cast her eyes around the slit of a room. 'You can't. Lorna, you can't live in this place after what you have been used to. And it's an awful area . . . You're right on the dock front. It's terrible.'

'Well, I can't see it from here. At the moment I just see those two people downstairs. They've been very kind.' After an awkward silence Lorna said, 'Would you tell Mr Stringer I'll come back to work on Monday? And would you mind telling him that if he hasn't got anyone else in my place I would like to withdraw my notice?'

A few minutes later, now dressed, she closed the front door on Faye and walked slowly back into the kitchen. She looked at the couple seated at the table and asked, 'Would you let me stay here for a while, Mrs Butting?'

'Well, lass, that's up to you, isn't it, Ned?' Mrs Butting jerked her head in her husband's direction.

'Aye, entirely, lass. It's up to you,' he echoed.

'Thank you.' Then, as she turned towards the staircase that went directly out of the room, she said, 'I'll get some place before your son returns.'

Mrs Butting's voice followed her as she went up the stairs, 'Well, you've got no need to make a move 'cos of him. His room's there waitin' and ready. You're puttin' nobody out. You stay as long as the fancy takes you.'

*   *   *

The fancy took Lorna for three months. She returned to number fifteen Pilot Street each night after a day at the office. As she stepped over the threshold into the cluttered, shining house and looked at the two people who were usually waiting for her, and at the table burdened with food, she knew a feeling of security and warmth that she had never experienced before.

Then one morning Mrs Butting received a letter. Holding it at a distance from her she said, 'Andrew's on his way back. Now I can't rightly make out the date, but I think it's the twenty-seventh. Is it, Dad?'

Mr Butting took the letter, and after looking at it for some time, said, 'Aye.'

That evening Lorna said, 'I must look out for a place.'

She felt hurt somehow when Mrs Butting's only remark was, 'Well, it's up to you, lass,' for she had longed for her to say, 'You'll do no such thing, you'll stay where you are.'

It was on a Friday, 16 June, that Lorna said, 'I think I've got a room, Mrs Butting.'

'Have you, lass?' Mrs Butting was polishing vigorously the top of the little sideboard. She was late finishing her housework this week as every window had been cleaned and fresh curtains hung, and everything in the house had been washed. Mrs Butting had explained that she was having one of her 'groundings'. As if, Lorna thought, she didn't ground the house every week. She watched her rubbing now at one small picture frame after another, all holding snaps of her lad in stages of his infancy. She had seen no picture of Mrs Butting's son as a man. At times she had wondered at this, but her innate politeness had checked any curious enquiry. One thing she did know: she did not want to meet this man. She felt she could not face him for he knew too much about her. Strangely, during the last few months, she had come to know quite a lot about him. Mrs Butting summed up all his qualities with 'He's the best lad on God's earth, there's none better.'

As if Mrs Butting were thinking this very thought at this moment she stroked the face beneath the glass as she said, 'If he'd been me own flesh and blood he wouldn't have been half as good, I know that.'

The words brought Lorna's attention sharply to the older woman and in undisguised surprise she said, 'But I thought he was your son, Mrs Butting?'

'No. No, lass.' Mrs Butting now moved across the kitchen and closed the door of the front room. Mr Butting had gone to bed early. Then, looking at Lorna, she said quietly, 'His mother wasn't seventeen when he was born. She threw herself into the docks. The bairn was left – he was a month old – so I took him.'

Threw herself into the docks! Not seventeen! And she had tried to throw herself into the docks too. And it was the baby of that young girl who had saved her. Life was strange.

Mrs Butting voiced this thought in the next

moment when she said, 'God works in funny ways. If He took me sight at this minute I wouldn't doubt Him. It would be for a purpose. All they found on the bairn was a little box, an' you know what's inside the box, don't you?'

It was the first time the box had been mentioned and Lorna said quietly, 'Yes, a miniature of the Ten Commandments.'

'Aye, a little book of the Ten Commandments. Well, all that bairn inherited was that little book. And I took it as an omen. You see, we couldn't have a child, me and Ned, and Ned was on the booze at the time, drinking himself blind. But, from the time the bairn came, well, things eased a bit. And then he went and fell down the ship's hold. He was a bit bottled at the time and he never got the use of his legs back. Strange thing to say, but it was a blessing. I worked for him and me lad. There was no compensation, 'cos they found the bottle in his pocket. Then the lad has worked for us.'

Lorna could say nothing. She went upstairs and held the little box in her hand for a long time, but when she opened it and the tiny pages fell apart and she read, 'Honour thy father and mother,' she snapped it closed again.

Saturday dinnertime she picked her way among the children playing in Pilot Street. After opening the front door she passed through the room and into the kitchen, and saw seated at the table, facing her, a strange man.

He got slowly to his feet and they looked at each other. 'Hello, there,' he said.

She remembered the voice from the night by the river. It was pure north-country, and in such contrast to his face that she had the impression someone else was speaking for him: by the look of him he should be speaking with a broken accent. Not with the lilt of a Frenchman, or the guttural twang of a German, but in the clipped way of the East. His eyes were a deep brown, his hair straight and black, his skin thick and creamy. He had what her mother would call . . . a touch of the tar brush. Slight, but unmistakably evident. Nasty! Don't touch! It was almost as if her mother was at her elbow, nudging her.

He was smiling at her, a wide, kind smile, waiting for her to speak.

'Hello,' she said.

Mrs Butting, slightly flushed, said quickly, 'I'm a daft individual. I thought he said he was coming on the twenty-seventh an' it was the seventeenth. Would you believe it?'

No, Lorna would not believe it. She knew that both Mr and Mrs Butting had purposely told her the wrong date so that she would be here when their lad arrived. And strangely, this lightened the heaviness in her heart. Mrs Butting had not been indifferent to her going; perhaps she even wanted her to stay. She looked at the man now as he did an unusual thing for someone brought up in Pilot Street: he had moved round the table and pulled a chair forward for her.

She did not take the proffered seat. Nor could she look at him as she said, 'Thank you, but I won't sit down yet. I'm rather hot, and would like to change.'

He said nothing but stood aside and allowed her to walk across the small space towards the stairs. When she reached them, Mrs Butting said, 'Did you get the room you went after?'

'Yes,' she replied.

There was a stillness. Then Mrs Butting said, 'The dinner will be on the table in a few minutes, lass.'

When she sat down on the side of her bed she was shivering from head to foot. And she kept repeating, 'Mrs Butting shouldn't have done it, she shouldn't.'

After having tea out and going to the pictures, she returned to the house about ten o'clock. In case Mr Butting had gone to bed she went up the dark narrow alley and round to the back. She opened the door quietly and went through the scullery. The man was sitting in Mr Butting's basket chair. He was in his shirtsleeves with his legs stretched out and his feet resting on the fender. He had a pipe in his mouth and he was writing something in an exercise book. At the sight of Lorna he rose quickly to his feet, saying, 'Oh, I thought it was me ma. She's just gone down to the Crofts, they're expecting a baby. Sit down, won't you?'

She could not make any excuse and sat, pulling

off her hat as she did so. When he was seated again he looked at her and, after a moment, asked quietly, 'How are you feeling?'

'Better. Much better. I – I've never thanked you.'

'There's no need.'

'I must return your . . . keepsake.'

'Thanks.' He laughed now, a gay sound, then leant forward and tapped out his pipe on the hob. 'You could never imagine what I've been through without it. I'm superstitious, you know.' Again came the laugh, and then he added, 'I expected our boat to blow up at any minute. I'm surprised to be here.'

She realised he was as nice as if he really was Mrs Butting's son. But she found that she could not look at his face for long, for the simple reason that she wanted to keep looking at it. His eyes drew hers. The deep warm depth of them, the sad depth of them, the laughing depth of them. All he was was mirrored in his eyes. She rose to her feet, and he said, 'Don't scamper away because of me.'

'I'm not.'

'Yes, you are . . . I'll not trouble you.'

'I wasn't thinking of that.' Her denial was strong. 'It's me who's the trouble.'

'Don't you believe it – you're no trouble. Ma's letters have been full of nothing else. You know, she thinks the world of you.'

'Does she?' She was looking sideways at him.

'She does that. It's meant a lot to her having you

here. And I wrote and told her to change my room over because you can't stay in that tiny one. But she wouldn't until I came back. Would you stay if you had a bigger room?'

'It isn't that.'

'What is it, then?'

'Oh, I don't know. It's . . . well . . .'

'It's me?'

'No! No!' The denial was vehement now. 'Why should it be?'

'Then why go? I can change over rooms the morrer; I'm used to narrow cabins. And, what's more, I'm not here for very long at a time.' He stood up and faced her. 'Will you tell her when she comes in that you're staying? She'll be over the moon if you do.'

She turned her eyes from his face and looked towards the dresser, and as she did so she knew why Mrs Butting had left no photographs around of her lad as a man. She was wise was Mrs Butting: she knew that you couldn't feel the impact of a personality through a picture, it had to come through flesh and blood; and when the personality was strong enough, what matter the flesh or the blood?

She started as his hands came on to her shoulders. His face was close to hers now. His eyes looked straight down into her thoughts as he said, 'You have nothing to fear from me. I won't trouble you. You must believe that.'

She hung her head as if in shame, and when he

released her she turned from him and groped blindly for the latch of the staircase door.

She was surprised to know the length of holidays that men working on tankers got. Also she was finding that Andrew Butting was changing her ideas of sailors. She had thought that most of them drank and hit the high spots while ashore, and perhaps some of them still did, but not Andrew or the shipmates he talked about. Most of them seemed to be studying for this or that promotion. Andrew's study was to get him his chief's ticket. She understood that he spent a good part of his day at the Marine Technical School up in the town.

Every evening, over the last three weeks, she had found him, on her return, in the kitchen, but tonight he was standing at the corner of Pilot Street, waiting for her.

'There's a man in the house wanting to see you. I thought you'd better know.'

'A man?' she repeated.

'He didn't give his name. He's fair, over six foot.'

'I'm not going in,' she said.

'I would if I were you. He'll keep coming until he sees you. He looks determined.'

'I can't, it's finished, I can't.'

He took her arm and led her down the street. 'Go in the back way,' he said. 'Ma and Da are in the front room. They've left the coast clear for you. Go on now and get it over. I'll wait out here.'

Charles was sitting stiffly on a straight-backed kitchen chair. He rose when she came into the room, and Lorna found that she could look at him and there was no pain.

He was deeply embarrassed, humble. 'Lorna. Oh, Lorna, I had to see you.'

'Why?'

'I've been mad, stark staring mad.'

'Has it fallen through, then?' Her voice sounded light and airy, but cold.

'I wasn't to blame altogether, believe me.'

'I do believe you.'

'I'll do anything – anything – to earn your forgiveness, Lorna. Anything in the world.'

'There is nothing in the world you can do for me, Charles.'

He stared at her, his lips working, twitching like an old man's. 'You loved me, Lorna, you know you did.'

'Yes, of course I loved you. That's why I promised to marry you, but I don't love you any longer.'

'Give me another chance, Lorna. Come out of here.' His voice dropped. 'Why are you here, anyway, in this place? What brought you here?'

'It's a fair question, Charles.' She did not lower her voice as he had. 'It was you brought me here, or sent me here. I tried to drown myself that night and would have succeeded but for these kind people.' She did not give the credit to Andrew alone.

He said slowly, 'Oh, no, Lorna.'

'Oh, yes, Charles.' Unconsciously she had mimicked him. 'And now, if you don't mind,' she said, 'Mr and Mrs Butting want to use their kitchen.'

'Lorna, look, you can't finish it like this. Come out with me . . . please. Somewhere where we can talk.'

'We have nothing more to talk about. I don't wish ever to see you again, Charles. All I wish is that sometime I will come to think of you kindly. I know there will be a time when I will be grateful to God that I didn't marry you.'

He picked up his hat from the table, then looked at her long and hard. 'You're changed, Lorna.'

'Of course, I am, Charles. And the person I am now would never suit you. I'm no longer pliable. You've had a lucky escape.' She found that she was smiling, and then she said, 'Would you mind going out the back way?' She preceded him into the scullery and, opening the door, she added, 'Go through that alley and you will find the street.'

He had crossed the step when he turned and looked at her once more, and again he said, 'Lorna?' but she closed the door in his face and stood with her back to it. She was no longer smiling, her heart was thumping under her ribs, there was a mist before her eyes and she felt faint.

She was standing with head bowed, supporting herself on the little table near the gas stove, when the door opened again and Andrew's voice came from behind her. 'Are you all right?'

She lifted her head and looked at the rough green-painted bricks, then turned towards him, her head bowed. 'Yes, I'm all right.'

'Sure?'

'Yes.'

'Do you think you've done the right thing?'

'I've done the right thing.'

His fingers came gently under her chin and lifted her face until her eyes met his. Then he said, 'Come on, let's have a cup of tea.'

Charles paid his visit on the Monday evening, and her mother came on the Thursday, the day before Andrew returned to his ship.

Lorna had just come in and was upstairs in her room, the room that had been Andrew's, changing her dress when Mrs Butting pushed open the door and whispered, 'Now, look, lass, take this easy. There's somebody downstairs, I'd say it was your mother. Now, now, don't get disturbed, just take it easy.'

'I'm not going down, Mrs Butting.'

'You must, lass. You must face this. You faced him, and if you can do that, you can face her. And after all, she's your mother.'

'I hold no sentimental theories about mothers, Mrs Butting. Some species kill their young.'

'Well, I don't know nowt about that, lass. Look, now, go down and get it over. If she's back in the town you'll run into each other some time or other. Go on now, there's a good lass.'

When Lorna went into the front room, Louise Harding was looking at the iron bed as if it were a reptile.

'Well? What do you want?'

Louise's mouth had a pathetic droop. Her beautifully made-up face was quivering, and her voice was a whimper. 'Oh, Lorna, don't be like that. I've come to apologise. It hasn't been easy, but I've come.'

'Charles was here on Monday.'

'Charles. Don't talk to me about Charles!' Her voice was bitter now. 'I must have been crazy. And let me tell you, my dear, you've had a lucky escape. I didn't really do you a bad turn, after all.'

'No, you didn't.'

'I've opened the house again.'

'Have you?'

'Your room is ready, Lorna. We could start all over again. We'd understand each other much better now.'

'I'm afraid that's out of the question. You know that you and I have nothing in common. We never had. You're on your own and you want company. Also my wages, of which you have availed yourself for years, must be more necessary than ever to you now.'

'How can you speak to me like that, Lorna? You know it isn't true. Good gracious, girl, you have changed. You're talking just like your father used to.'

'I'm glad to hear that.'

Louise Harding closed her eyes and joined her hands together, pressing them into her breast dramatically as she said, 'I didn't come here to quarrel. I came because I want you back, Lorna.'

'I'm not coming back. Nothing you could say would induce me to.'

'You mean you'd rather live here in this?' Louise spread her arms wide. 'It's shocking. I don't know how you ever found such a place.'

Lorna did not enlighten her mother with the facts of how she had come to live at number fifteen Pilot Street, for at that moment the conversation was cut off by the front door opening and Andrew entering the room. He halted and glanced quickly at them. Then, inclining his head towards the older woman, he said, 'Good evening.'

Louise made no answer. As the man moved past her and went into the other room, her horrified gaze lifted from him and came to rest on Lorna. 'Who is that man?'

'He is Mrs Butting's son.'

'You can't go on living here, Lorna,' Louise hissed.

'Why not?'

'Do I need to explain?'

'No.' Lorna had seen that when her mother's eyes fell on Andrew they had spoken the old phrase: Nasty! Don't touch!

She said now, hissing as her mother had, 'Don't you dare say a word against him. You don't know him. He's a wonderful man and you're welcome to Charles.'

'Lorna – you are not . . . !'

'Living with him? Is that what you want to know? Well, I'm not going to enlighten you. You can ponder over it for yourself. And now I want you to go, and I don't want to see you again. My life is my own and I'm going to use it as I think fit.'

'You're hard – hard and wicked.'

' "Oh, would the giftie the good Lord gie us." Father used to quote that to you often, didn't he? Goodbye, Mother. I hope you'll be happy.'

There was no look of contrition now on Louise Harding's face as she looked at her daughter. Then she spoke some terrible words. Yet the words in themselves freed Lorna, for Louise Harding said, 'I hate you! I think I've hated you since the day you were born. I never wanted you. And when you came he could see nothing else.'

'I know that. I think I've always known it. Goodbye, Mother.'

When the front door closed the kitchen door opened and Mrs Butting came into the room, saying, 'Oh, my God, lass!'

Lorna knew that every word had been heard in the kitchen. She bowed her head and said now, 'I'm all right, Mrs Butting. Don't worry.'

'Come and sit down, lass. Come and have something to eat.' It was Mrs Butting's remedy for all ills. 'You're as white as a sheet. Sit down, there, it's over. Don't worry.' She patted Lorna into her place at the table. Andrew was sitting opposite, and to the side was Mr Butting. They were both looking at her. She raised her eyes and looked from one to the other, her gaze resting on Andrew as she said softly, 'It's all right. I'm all right, don't worry.' And the men began to eat.

The meal was nearing its end and hardly a word had been exchanged when Lorna, looking across the table directly into the waiting brown eyes, said, 'There's a play on in town that I'd like to see. Would you take me, Andrew?'

Andrew returned his cup to the saucer, glanced at the chestnut hair, the oval face, then looked deep into the grey eyes. 'I'd be pleased to, Lorna.'

Mrs Butting rose hastily from the table and, going towards the fire, she leant her arm on the brass rod. Lowering her head on to it, she began to cry.

When Andrew put his arms around her and drew her tight against him, Mr Butting put out his hand and touched Lorna's. He patted it for some seconds before saying in a thick voice, 'She always cries at the good things an' laughs at the bad.'

Half an hour later when Lorna walked out of the front door with Andrew, a lot of people were about in Pilot Street and they smiled at them and said, 'Hello, there.'

When they had gone a little way, Lorna shyly put the tips of her fingers into the crook of Andrew's right arm where they hovered tentatively for a few seconds until the fingers of Andrew's other hand found them and drew them into a more secure position. And when they were settled he pressed them firmly and looked down at her. Then he looked ahead, walking with chin up and shoulders back, a fine figure of a man.

And now there flowed through Lorna a joy as strong and fresh as the wind blowing in from the North Sea. And like Mrs Butting, who was standing on the doorstep watching them, she knew that God worked in strange ways.

8

For Fear Of . . .

Charles Stanley closed the front door behind him, walked the six paces to the foot of the stairs, and paused. Except on Sundays, he had done the same thing practically every day for the past nine years. Whether he entered the house at five o'clock, half past six, or even ten o'clock, as he sometimes did on a Saturday night, Mrs Brownlow's door would open and she would make some remark, such as 'Got back, then?' or 'Well, here we are again.' He had long ceased to make any verbal return to his landlady's profound statements, but would answer them with a movement of his head, either a lift of his chin, a nod, or a jerk to the side. Then looking upwards, he would mount the steep stairs to the first landing, turn the corner, and continue to the second floor. By this time his eyes would be cast downwards, and, like a knowledgeable blind man, he would walk to one of the two doors opposite the stairhead. Sometimes he entered by the left-hand one, and sometimes by the one on the right. It didn't matter. The left-hand one led into his sitting-room-cum-bedroom, and the right-hand one into his kitchen-cum-bathroom – the bath had a lid on it, which acted as a table. There was another door on the landing. It was the main door to this supposedly self-contained flat, but it was now more than six years since he had gone through it.

However, he was still at the foot of the stairs and he blinked as if coming out of a light doze. Slowly, he turned his head to look towards Mrs Brownlow's door. It was closed. For the first time in this long, past-reviving, respect-dwindling day, his mind lifted from himself and he thought, Where is she? The answer did not come to him that she might be out. If she went out, and he supposed she must, it would never be after five o'clock at night. But this wasn't five o'clock, it was twenty minutes past three. Even so, because she knew where he had been, he had expected her to be at the door, not with just her dew-lapped face poking round it, but standing squarely outside in the hall, and saying, this time, 'Well, you've got it over. Was she buried or cremated?' And he would have answered, 'Cremated.'

Odd, when you came to think about it, not knowing before whether your wife was to be buried or cremated.

But where was his landlady? He bent his long thin body in the direction of the door. There seemed to be someone talking in the distance. That would mean whoever it was was important enough to get past the kitchen.

As he climbed the stairs the emptiness in him deepened. All the way back, sitting next to the driver of the hearse who had kindly offered him a lift into town, he had thought, If I'd only someone to talk it over with, but there'll only be her. She's the only one who knows, and yet I can't talk to her. But, anyway, she'd be there waiting for him with her set clipped sentences, and that would be something. But like everything in his life, nothing turned out the way he imagined it would.

When he reached the second landing he stopped for a moment and drew a deep breath, as a man does when he has to fortify himself against a coming test. But he was only going towards his own sitting-room door. After opening it, he stood there, his slightly greying hair within a few inches of the lintel, and looked about him. It did not take long, although the room seemed crowded with the single hard chair, the armchair, the two-foot-square table, the single divan, and the sideboard. It was on the sideboard that his eyes came to rest, on the conglomeration of articles that covered its small top. Having closed the door behind him and automatically laid down his hat and taken off his overcoat, he moved forward, his eyes still on the sideboard. Now he walked towards it and picked up a photograph, groped backwards towards the hard chair and sat down heavily. It was as if the picture of the woman within the frame still had the power to make him cower inwardly.

He looked down at the face with its bright dark eyes, straight strong nose, and full lips. May had been good-looking, beautiful in a way. She had once said to him, in one of her rare playful moods,

'We're a handsome pair, you and I, and we're going places.' She had wanted so badly to go places. Not just walking around London and looking at places. That cost nothing. She wanted to go places that cost money. That phrase 'go places' held the clue to his life of failure. It sounded so ordinary, but its meaning was deep and complex. And May had chosen the wrong man to achieve it.

He had been twenty-four when he met May. Within six months they were married, and from their wedding day May took up her mission, which was to change him, and in changing him make something of him. She had tried, God knows she had tried; and he had tried, God knew that also. But the mission was doomed from its birth. Failure in his case had been given many names, laziness . . . lack of guts . . . inferiority . . . no ambition, but never was it put down to timidity or bad luck. Yet it was those two things, and those two only, that had foiled May's plans, for Charles had been born timid, and luck, good luck, is reluctant to follow timidity.

He was fourteen when he first faced the fact that he was frightened inside, and this had made him join a gang. But he had been unable to force himself to stay in it for fear of . . . Those words had preceded every action of his life, for fear of this, for fear of that. In this first case it had been for fear that he would suddenly vomit at some of the things the lads got up to, especially when they went ratting or catting.

By the time he met May he had been in six jobs

and had left each because . . . for fear of. Fear of a workmate who was helping himself to the stock: he hadn't wanted to split, or get involved. Then it was for fear of a foreman who had eyes that saw through him, and used his fear to bully him. And so it had gone on, until he met May.

It was strange, but the very quality that had finally separated them had, in the beginning, been the attraction for May. 'I'm going to turn you back to front,' she had said. 'You're no longer going to be Charles Stanley, but Stanley Charles, as tough as you're long.' She had punched him playfully in the chest, and he had grabbed at her hand, as he had grabbed at the idea.

In this, at least, May succeeded in part. Charles Stanley became Stanley Charles. And Stanley Charles was a fearless individual who stood before the wardrobe mirror and talked. He talked and talked to the bold reflection. However, the reflection never came to life. It was imprisoned in the glass. But over the years he went on talking: 'Now look here, Pedleston, I've been with the firm seventeen years. They've left me at this end because I know the ropes, so don't you start giving me orders. I'm here to see to the booking, your job is to check the loading. See that you stick to it.'

The day Stanley Charles made that bold statement to the image in the mirror, his sixteen-year-old son had said to him, 'You've got as much drive as a snail with polio. Why don't you have some guts and go to the head office and tell them they can't put Pedleston over you, especially when there's only the two of you? Strewth! If I'd been with them as long as you, I'd be running the whole damn brewery by now, not left behind in a rat-eaten warehouse. God! It's no wonder me mam eats you up.'

After this May did not continue to eat him up for much longer. Four weeks to be exact. One night he returned home and there was Mrs Brownlow waiting for him at the foot of the stairs. 'She's gone,' she said, 'and taken the lot with her.'

As he had walked from one starkly empty room to another, his sense of failure had been so devastating that he had the weird impression his body was shrinking. When he could speak he had asked, 'Did she leave any message?'

Mrs Brownlow had blinked at him and run her furred tongue around her lips, saying, 'She said she'd come to your funeral.'

The shrinking feeling had increased. Then Mrs Brownlow had said, 'If you want to stay you may. It was two flats before, it can be two again, and I've a few bits and pieces downstairs you can have.'

He had stayed because he had to have some sort of anchor, and the flat and Mrs Brownlow were the only things in this vast, impersonal universe that he could hold on to.

Some weeks later, when he was beginning to accept his new situation, Stanley Charles had made one last appearance. He had looked in the shaving mirror above the sink and said, 'You're free. Don't you realise that? You're only forty-one and you're free. You can go anywhere. Do anything. Get going, Stanley Charles!'

But he hadn't . . . for fear of what would happen to Charles Stanley. Charles Stanley had got used to being a clerk, and such jobs, at his age, were not all that easy to come by.

His life had fallen into a routine that had become almost as inconspicuous as his breathing. Every evening he tidied the two rooms and prepared his evening meal – the only real meal of the day. On Saturday afternoon he walked around some particular part of London, and in the evening he went to the pictures. Once he had tried getting drunk, but afterwards had felt so ill he had not again resorted to this type of oblivion. On Sundays he never went out, because he always felt more lonely outside on a Sunday. He had his radio, his books, and he had taken up marquetry.

Then last Saturday he had received the telegram. 'Mother died yesterday. Funeral Monday 11.30 Tafflings, Croydon. Jim.'

He was swimming once more in a sea of guilt and remorse, and his timidity was dragging him down. Her last message to him had been 'I'll come to your funeral.' She had been bitter, had May, and he had a strong feeling that she had died in bitterness.

This feeling had been borne out when, a few hours ago, he had met his son. They had come together like strangers, in fact he had hardly recognised him, for there was nothing of himself to be seen in Jim. But from his son's first words he knew that May was not dead. With open reluctance, Jim had introduced his wife; and was it just a strange coincidence that the girl looked almost like May had years ago? Perhaps it wasn't so strange when you came to think of it. But one thing was certain, the girl would have no need to . . . eat Jim up; Jim was already eating himself up. This did nothing to lighten his sense of guilt.

He rose now from the chair and put the photo back on its allotted space on the sideboard, then went into the kitchen, put the kettle on the gas stove and set the tray. Tonight he would make no meal; although he'd had nothing since breakfast time he didn't feel hungry.

It was as he took the tray into the other room that he heard the front door bang. This was followed by Mrs Brownlow's weighty tread on the stairs; and he stood by the table waiting for her knock. When it came, he called immediately, 'Come in.'

'Well! Get it over? What was it?'

'She was cremated.'

'Oh, cremated . . . Huh! Well, that's over. At this minute she'll be where the good God pleases, and you're still here. And you know what you want to do?'

'No, Mrs Brownlow.'

'Burn that picture!' She pointed to the sideboard. 'And his too. He wouldn't hang on to yours, I bet, unless he's changed some. Has he?'

'I don't think so, Mrs Brownlow.'

'No, he wouldn't. And now get yourself out, see a bit of life. She's gone. She can't hang over you any more . . . Oh, by the way, I've let the flat next door.' She jerked her head. 'She won't trouble you. Married . . . God knows how.'

'Children?' he asked anxiously: twice in the past six years there had been children living in the flat next door, and it was as if they had been living in the same room with him, the shouting, the yelling, the crying . . . and, worst of all, the quarrelling between the parents.

'No. Just as well too, I'd say. Well, there it is. She moves in at the weekend. You won't see much of her. Well, that's it. Get your tea now; then do what I tell you, burn those photos.'

He drank his tea, but he didn't burn the photos.

If Mrs Brownlow hadn't told him that the flat next door was let, he would have thought that the muffled sounds, which came to him at long intervals, were from a family of mice that had taken possession.

His neighbour had been installed for nearly three weeks when Mrs Brownlow, bringing him to his usual pause at the foot of the stairs, kept him a minute longer than usual by asking, 'Well, what's your opinion?'

'Opinion?'

'About her.' She rolled her eyes upwards.

'I haven't met her.'

'No? Well, not surprised. You'll know what I mean when you do. Queer, all round. Said to her, "You a widow?" and know what she said? "My husband isn't dead." Queer way to answer. Not yes or no but "My husband isn't dead!" Funny, wasn't it?'

'Yes.'

'Go an' get your tea.'

He lifted his eyes upwards and ascended the stairs.

It was the following Sunday that he first saw the woman, and he knew what Mrs Brownlow meant. He was sitting reading when his head lifted from the book and he listened to a movement outside his door. It could have been a step, yet seemed too faint for one. When no knock came he went on with his reading, until a few minutes later there was the sound again. When he took the two steps from the chair and opened the door it was to see the back of a woman bent down towards the floor. He could see the top of her head, and her hands outstretched holding the cat, then she straightened up.

Later, when thinking about it, he considered that he had managed the situation well, for he had smiled into the woman's face as he said, 'It's a nice cat, but I suppose you have trouble keeping it in?'

'It isn't mine. I thought it belonged to you. I've kept bringing it back.'

She was tall: their eyes were on a level and he made himself look right back into them so that his own wouldn't wander round her face. 'No, it isn't mine. I'm out all day; it wouldn't be fair to an animal.'

'No.' She looked at the cat again and, jerkily, she bent down and lifted it into her arms, where it evidently considered it belonged for it immediately tucked its head under her chin. 'I'll keep it if it will stay.'

'Oh, it will stay.' He widened his smile.

'Thank you.' She made a single downward movement with her head before turning from him and crossing the narrow landing to her door.

Back in the room he did not sit down and resume his reading but stood looking towards the wall that separated the two rooms . . . God, it must be awful for a woman to have skin like that. It looked like thick dried leather that had been dyed a pinkish-red. It made her appear like someone badly disfigured, yet she wasn't disfigured, not in the accepted sense. Her nose was quite all right, a bit short at the end, but that was considered an advantage with some women. And her mouth on anyone else would have been attractive, for it was full and had some shape to it. A really ugly woman could sometimes appear quite attractive . . . Look at Miss Spencer who used to run the canteen. But she – he blinked towards the wall – was not ugly-attractive, she was just ugly. It was that skin, and there was little or nothing, he supposed, she could do about it. Her eyes might have been a redeeming feature for they were a nice deep brown, but their expression spoiled them.

As he continued to stare at the wall he thought about this expression. He wanted to put a name to it. He felt he recognised that particular look, yet he couldn't place the source from which it was derived.

He sat down. What did she do all the time so quietly behind that wall? He must quiz Mrs Brownlow . . . That was Stanley Charles talking;

Charles Stanley would never ask Mrs Brownlow any questions about the woman.

As he turned from his contemplation of the wall he looked at May's photograph. May had had beautiful skin. Strange, when he thought of it, that May, with enough poison and bitterness in her to eat like acid through iron, could have had beautiful skin.

He went out into the kitchen and set about making his tea, and as he did so he remembered something else about the woman, and it seemed to him very surprising . . . She had a nice voice. When he came to think of it he'd never heard any woman speak like her. It was a cultured voice; but that wasn't what he remembered about it. It had some quality and, like the look in her eyes, he couldn't find a name to describe it.

A month passed and he heard nothing louder than the mouse noises from the next room, but he learnt that his close neighbour's name was Manners. Mrs Brownlow had given him this information. Also that she performed the unusual service of a rhyme writer. 'Doing them poetry bits for Christmas cards and the like,' was how Mrs Brownlow had described her occupation, and she had added, 'Never credit it, would you?'

No, he never would have credited it.

It was during one bitterly cold night that he was woken by the sound of coughing. He was startled by the fact that it was near his head. He must have been aware of it for some time in his sleep even though the sound was muffled, as if she was coughing under the bedclothes. He felt he could put out his hand and touch her. The thought was slightly embarrassing, as if she were in the same bed. He had not known her bed was on the other side of the wall. He would have thought she used that room as a sitting room. Did she hear him moving in the night? Likely. The coughing was louder now, and hard. She sounded as if she were choking. Then the sound grew fainter. She must have got up and gone into the other room. He looked at his watch. It said ten minutes past one. How long had she been coughing like that? As it was Saturday night he had been out until after ten. He remembered now that he had heard a muffled cough when he had come home at dinnertime.

At two o'clock he got up and made himself a hot drink. The coughing was still coming from the far room. At half past three he was standing fully dressed on the landing, wondering whether he should go down and wake Mrs Brownlow. It was unlikely she would hear the coughing, far away in her burrow. She had never heard the children, or their parents when they quarrelled.

When he stood outside the door that had once been his, the sound was so harsh that he found his own chest muscles contracting. He tapped on the door.

The coughing stopped, then started again, and he knocked much louder this time. When she opened the door she was still coughing. 'I'm – sorry, I'm—'

'Look,' his hand was out towards her, 'don't

worry. Don't fret yourself. I just wondered . . . can I get you something?'

She had her hands on her chest, gripping large folds of her dressing-gown – which, he noticed, was a smart affair – and she gasped, in painful breaths, 'The – the doctor, in – the – morning.'

'You'll want some medicine before then. Have you any friar's balsam?'

She shook her head.

'Well, I think I've got a drop left in a bottle. You go in. I'll get it.' He moved his hand towards her again but did not touch her. Ten minutes later his hands touched her hair as he placed the towel over her head, and said, 'Now breathe deeply if you can.'

As her tortured breathing came from under the towel he looked about him. He had never seen the flat look like this. May had thought she had taste, she used to brag about it – but this was different. None of the pieces of furniture matched, yet things mingled, as May's setpieces never had. And why? Because, he supposed, these were all old things, nearly all antiques, he would say.

When she lifted her head from the basin her face looked as if it had been boiled. He gazed down at her with pity as he asked, 'Have you any lemons?' She nodded, got up and went towards the kitchen. When she had a lemon in her hand he said, 'Let me.'

The drink had little or no effect on the cough and he said, 'I should get into bed and keep warm.'

She answered, between gasps, 'It's worse . . . better up . . . Please . . . I'm sorry to . . . to disturb you.'

'No. Now, don't worry. I don't sleep half the night. Look, I'll go and make a cup of tea. And it will soon be light. If you're no easier then, I'll phone a doctor.'

She lifted her head and looked at him, and the expression in her eyes blotted out the rest of her face: their brown was deepened almost to black with gratitude, like those of an animal whose pain had been eased. No-one had ever looked at him with gratitude. If he had performed services, and he had, that deserved gratitude, they had been taken for granted. He could never remember being thanked with such a wealth of gratitude. And what had he done for this woman to deserve that look?

As he stood in his own kitchen and made the tea, the source of that other expression in her eyes, which he had seen that first morning when he had met her, came to him, and he was surprised that he hadn't been able to name it before, for God knew he was well acquainted with it . . . The name of the expression was timidity, and its source was . . . for fear of.

At five o'clock he rang a doctor, and he came at six. He was brusque. It was Sunday morning and he'd had a late Saturday night. After seeing Mrs Manners he stood on the landing, looked coldly up at Charles's stooped length and stated, 'Bronchial . . . bad. You'll have to be careful with her. Keep her in bed. You shouldn't have let her get up. Touch of pneumonia . . . a little on the lung. I'll look in tomorrow.'

He was gone and Charles knew he should have said, 'I'm not her husband.' But the man had intimidated him. He was the kind of individual who might have replied, with a calculating look in his eye, 'What are you, then?'

The doctor had left a prescription, and later Charles walked for over an hour, trying to find a chemist who was open for medicine on a Sunday morning. He felt he couldn't keep her hanging on until six that evening without some relief.

When he returned at eleven o'clock Mrs Brownlow's door was open: it was evident she had just got up. 'Oh, it's you,' she said. 'Been out?'

'Mrs Manners took ill,' he said, 'in the night.' He knew that his face was flushed. 'I – I heard her . . . coughing all the time. I was going to come for you, but didn't want to disturb you. I wouldn't have gone in otherwise.'

She looked at him for a long moment then said, with what for her was a smile, 'No, you wouldn't.'

It didn't sound unkind, but it made him feel like some sort of a worm . . . or perhaps just like Charles Stanley, and Charles Stanley wasn't the kind of fellow who would go into a woman's room uninvited – or even when he *was* invited.

Mrs Brownlow made no mention of coming upstairs to see Mrs Manners, but when he had reached the third step, she remarked, 'I don't think she's entitled to the Mrs. All her mail is addressed Miss. And there was a card from her father. Looks as if he's got married and, judging by her, he'll be no chicken, for she won't see forty again.'

It was a strange Sunday. The strangest Charles thought he had experienced in his life. The flat seemed to have become one again. By the end of the long day he had lost count of the times he had crossed the landing.

It was ten o'clock when he said, with a magical familiarity, 'There, now, you'll have a better night. That medicine's telling already.'

She was propped up in bed. It was a single bed with a very nice cover, which matched her quilted bed jacket. It was odd how she had surrounded herself with pretty things to suit a pretty woman. Perhaps she had bought them to match her voice. That was a thought: perhaps she had.

He was standing some way from her when he spoke. Since his hands had touched her hair, he had tried, except when he was putting the hot drinks on the bedside table, to keep his distance. But now, across that distance, she thrust her hand. It was an impulsive tentative gesture, and as it hung wavering in the air, an expression he recognised returned to her eyes, an expression so akin to the feeling that had ruled and ruined his own life. Like a poor swimmer trying to save a life, his hand was thrust out and grasped hers tightly. The fingers entwined with his and the two hands held long after the expression in her eyes had changed.

That was all, no words.

9

Silly Mid-on

It was Sheila who brought the nagging matter to a climax in Betty's mind. She had been running backwards and forwards between the kitchen and the hall, then into the garden, from the time she had got up, shouting, 'Silly mid-on! Silly mid-on! LBW! Square-leg! Silly mid-on!' When Peter came downstairs, lifted her high above his head and, whirling her round and round in the tiny hall, shouted with her, 'Silly mid-on! Silly mid-on!' the whole cause of Betty's discontent rushed to the fore and to her lips, and she banged down a saucepan of milk on the stove and screamed, 'Stop it! Stop it! Both of you.'

They stopped it so suddenly that the subsequent silence screamed as loudly as the noise had in Betty's ears. And when they stood in the kitchen doorway, the little redhead and the tall redhead, and gazed at her, she gulped and drew in a great breath as if she had been choking.

The milk was running over the stove and dribbling on to the floor, the sun was streaming across the checked breakfast cloth and the array of shining coloured crockery, dusting everything with yellow, and Betty stared back at her husband and daughter with angry eyes while her thoughts raced over old ground: I'm not going to put up with it. I'm not! I'm not! It's every Saturday alike: cricket, cricket. It was bad enough when he played on a Sunday, but now Saturday too, week after week. Well, she wasn't going to stand for it and she would tell him so. Now. The sooner the better.

But as Betty opened her mouth to tell him so her words were stopped as they were about to spill from her lips by the expression on Peter's face, which was changing from startled enquiry to blankness. At the sight of this familiar look, Betty cried within herself, It isn't fair, he's going to close up again and I'll not be able to say a thing. Why can't we have this matter out? If only, she thought, he would get into a temper. But he refused to indulge in this outlet, and against his forbidding barrier of silence she felt, as always, helpless.

She had first experienced the power of this blank silence when she protested laughingly about his Sunday cricket. He had not made any retort, funny or otherwise, had just gazed at her, and his eyes had taken on a weird hooded look. Then, a few days later, she had been both hurt and infuriated when he told her that in future he was also going to play on a Saturday. It was as if, after some thought, he had done this in deliberate defiance. Yet it was so unlike Peter to be defiant: he was so easy-going, so lovable and kind. At least, he had been until then. But since that day the hooded look had come again and again to his face and had somehow formed a barrier between them, which was growing wider each week. She had only to suggest doing something different on a Saturday and the barrier was up.

Saturday after Saturday she had gone dutifully to watch him play. Hot days, cold days, windy days, she had sat knitting innumerable garments, becoming bored to extinction and irritated beyond measure with other wives, who followed the game with apparently avid interest – laid on for the occasion, Betty thought.

What irritated her more than anything else, however, was that her three-year-old daughter had picked up the cricket jargon, and, because Peter encouraged her, she jabbered it from morning till night.

Yet there had been times, Betty admitted to herself, when her interest had been sparked and promised some relief from the boredom. These were when Peter was batting and making a good score. She had found herself sitting up and taking notice when he was eighty not out. But that didn't happen often. At other times, for instance two Saturdays running, he had gone out for a duck and on the third Saturday had missed an easy catch, which allowed the other side to win by a couple of runs. Then it always seemed such a waste of time, although these particular incidents hadn't affected Peter. His reaction had been 'It's all in the game.'

All in the game! And what she would like to do with that game if only she had her way!

Now all she had to look forward to on this lovely, bright sunny day was a stuffy twenty-mile bus ride to play a little village team. She would have to sit on a bench, if she was lucky – it was usually the grass – for hours on end, then be expected to enjoy strong tea, bread and jam and buns, followed by more sitting, more knitting, more boredom.

What was sometimes even worse than the game was the bus ride home, for the match did not stop when the game was over – no: you got it step by step, ball by ball, in the bus, on and on.

She had asked Peter yesterday if he couldn't cut the cricket today and take them to the sea, but he had replied stiffly that the side was short of players and he couldn't let them down at short notice.

He hadn't suggested her taking Sheila and going on her own. Perhaps he had realised she might submit this alternative to him for he had put in quickly, 'Sheila likes cricket, and she'll get as much fresh air there.'

Not a word about her. Presumably she didn't count.

She lifted Sheila on to her chair, and under her mother's unusual sharpness the child became subdued. She glanced at her father for sympathy but he, too, looked stern and not silly mid-onish now. She pushed away her breakfast and started to whimper.

At this point the front-door bell rang. Peter rose from the table and went into the hall. He was gone only a moment or so before he returned, reading a letter. Betty resisted asking who it was from, for his face was growing stiffer and stiffer as he came to the end. Then, throwing it on to the table in her direction, he exclaimed tersely, 'It's from Mum and Dad. They want to come for a week.'

Betty picked it up and as she read it her thoughts were brought again to her own grievance. Well, if they came he'd have to stay at home for at least one weekend, so she would have some compensation for the bother of changing the rooms round. She forced herself to adopt an even tone as she remarked, 'That will be nice. They've never been to stay since we moved here.' Then, seeing his expression, she said tartly, 'Why? Don't you want them to come? You certainly don't look very pleased about it.'

'Do you want me to put flags out or something? Of course I want them to come. If I had waxed enthusiastic you'd only have said, "Oh, you can be cheerful when your people are coming."'

'Oh, that isn't fair!' she burst out. 'You know I've never said a thing like that.'

'Oh, well, what does it matter?' His brows were meeting and the barrier was up again.

They had gone in the stuffy little bus, and she had sat on the grass – no benches – and she had watched Peter stay in batting for most of the afternoon for a total score of twenty-nine. 'Stopping the rot', they called it. He had gone in after four men were out for seven. The captain had said, 'Cut in there, Peter, and see if you can stop the rot.' He had spoken as if a battle raged and the town's fall was imminent.

Peter had gone in, and stayed in, and all for twenty-nine runs, while other men got forty-five, fifty, with the last man fifty-two not out.

She wouldn't have cared, she thought, if he had done something to show for the afternoon's effort. But letting balls go past him, patting them gently, why, even Sheila could have hit them harder, she thought. She knew that this kind of play would be termed 'saving the side'. Saving the side! Oh, the childishness of it all.

In the bus home it was 'Good old Peter', 'Stonewall Peter', 'We showed 'em, thanks to old Peter.'

Old Peter! She had the urge to dash among all these eternal boys and knock their heads together.

The week that followed was one of strain between them. Obviously Peter wasn't looking forward to his parents' visit. Betty had met her in-laws only twice, the first time for a brief weekend before their marriage, the second at the actual wedding: Peter's work had kept him in Sussex and his parents had moved from the Midlands to Scotland, a distance which had seemed too far to take a young baby, so they had not yet seen Sheila.

Peter had always spoken of his father with affection, but about his mother he had been strangely reticent. Betty's impression of her mother-in-law remained that of a capable, jolly woman, and she thought of his father as kindly, vague, somehow withdrawn. She remembered she had caught him looking at her searchingly a number of times during their short acquaintance, and words of his came back to her now: 'Peter has the makings of a fine cricketer – he loves the game. Do you like cricket?' He had asked the question somewhat anxiously.

She had been about to answer, 'Yes,' when his wife had butted in: 'Well, I've never stopped Peter playing, have I? I've always said that would be some other woman's worry.'

Betty had thought, She must have been listening, and she remembered that Peter's father had risen sharply and walked away, looking more secretive and withdrawn than ever.

Well, his mother had been right: it was some other woman's worry and it was going to be the cause of serious trouble between her and Peter, so serious that she woke in the night thinking, I could get my old job back and my mother would have Sheila, then he could play every night of the week if he wanted to. She had rammed the corner of the sheet into her mouth to smother the sound of her weeping, and she had been sure that Peter was awake and aware of her tears for she felt him turn swiftly on to his side towards her. But he had checked himself and his arm had not come round her . . .

His parents arrived on Friday. Peter had got off early and gone to the station to meet them. She had stayed behind, getting the tea prepared and Sheila spruced up for her introduction to her grandparents.

They were very much as she remembered them, in fact so true had been her impressions that it seemed like yesterday that she had first met them.

They both adored Sheila on sight, but Sheila's affection was directed straight away towards her grandfather and, after tea, sitting on his knee, she confided to him her great tragedy. She had lost her cat. Did he know she had lost her cat?

No, and he was terribly sorry. 'Oh, we'll have to get you another Tiddles,' he said.

'Not Tiddles, Square-leg.'

'Square-leg!' Her grandfather was suddenly laughing, a free kind of laugh. 'That's good. You're a cricketer, eh?'

'No, I'm not a cricketer,' Sheila corrected him. 'Daddy is the cricketer. I just go and watch. Daddy's the best cricketer in the world. Do you think Square-leg will come back, Granddad?'

'Yes, he'll come back all right. They usually do.'

'She's a missis, not a man.'

'Oh! She's a missis, is she? Well, she's sure to come back, then.'

'When?'

'Oh, very soon. Come on, let's go into the garden and have a look for her, eh?'

They went off hand in hand, leaving Betty and Peter's mother alone in the dining room. Peter was already in the garden, weeding, and Betty felt wilder with him than ever for he had scarcely spoken at all during tea, making the atmosphere unnecessarily strained.

Betty was recalled to herself by Peter's mother saying, 'You're looking as pretty as ever. Housework and a baby haven't altered you.'

Gratefully, she turned to her mother-in-law. 'That's nice of you, but I have altered. You don't remain the same. Nobody does.' Her eyes were drawn towards the garden, and Mrs Davenport, looking at her shrewdly, spoke one word. 'Cricket?' she said.

Startled, Betty turned to her. 'What?'

'Oh, you don't have to tell me, my dear. I saw it the moment I came in.' She bent forward and wagged her finger at her daughter-in-law. 'My dear, you're going through what I went through. He's just like his father was at his age, cricket mad. But I cured him.' She lay back in her chair and laughed softly. 'I gave him his choice. The cricket bat or me, I said. I stuck it for a whole season, then I gave him my ultimatum. But you, my dear, have left it a bit late. Nevertheless, I'd put my foot down and keep it down. You've only got to stick it out and he'll toe the line all right.'

Betty looked at her mother-in-law smugly tapping her fingers together, and a strange feeling came over her as she asked, 'Has Dad never played cricket since the first year of your marriage?'

'Never, and what's more he's rarely been to a match since. I always have plans made for the weekend. That's my secret, my dear. Plan your weekend and make sure the plans can't be carried out without him.'

'Before you were married did you know he played cricket?' Betty asked.

'Of course I did. It was at the cricket club I got to know him. I wanted him, so I went to the matches to see him play.'

She laughed at this, and to Betty it didn't sound a jolly laugh any more.

'There's quite a lot of truth in the saying "All's fair in love and war", my dear. You see I never liked cricket, and all that sitting, hour after hour, got me down. Anyway, I knew which he would choose once he had to.'

Remembering her father-in-law's secret, withdrawn look, Betty thought, He's lost something – he's pathetic. Oh, she's been cruel. Then, quite suddenly, she found she was asking herself a question: What had she done? Then, loudly in her head, she was crying, Peter! Oh, Peter, I must never grow like this. Like her. And yet I have. Oh, Peter!

Sheila's high piping screech came through the open windows: 'Silly mid-on! Silly mid-on! LBW! Granddad.'

Betty turned quickly to the open window and saw Sheila with her tiny bat in her hands at one end of the lawn and her father-in-law bowling from the other. She saw him take four running strides, give a little jump, then his arm whirled and the ball came gently to Sheila's bat. But he wasn't bowling to Sheila. Looking at his face, Betty was amazed at the change in it. It had come to life. He was behind the stumps, determined to get the wicket. One wicket after another was falling before his eyes. Oh, Betty thought, with painful tenderness, he looks just like Peter. Oh, it's a shame. How could she?

'Square-leg! Square-leg!' screamed Sheila, digging up clumps of lawn in her efforts to hit the ball to the man who had momentarily become lost in the past.

'You see what I mean?' Mrs Davenport's voice

came from behind Betty. 'Even now he'd take it up – at his age. The war is never over against cricket, my dear. Remember what I said to you, be firm, put your foot down and keep it there.'

'Where is the blanco?'

They both turned quickly towards the door and Peter. He stood there with his white boots in his hand. He was looking at Betty with the closed look that made his face appear suddenly old, unlike his father's at this moment – it was as if they had changed places.

'There's a new one in the cupboard under the sink.'

'Well, he's pleasant,' said his mother. 'Like father, like son.'

Turning and looking at her mother-in-law, Betty had to restrain herself from shouting, 'Oh, be quiet, woman, I'm not going to make my Peter like you've made his father. There are limits. Are you blind to what you've done?' But all she said was, 'I'll go and find the blanco for him, he can never find anything.'

And, she thought, as she hurried out, I must tell him something else. I must tell him I have found out something about myself.

But when she reached the kitchen her father-in-law was there too, and it was he who greeted her. 'This young lady wants to show me the park, Betty. Is it too far for her to go?'

Looking from Mr Davenport to Peter's stiff back, Betty said, 'No, it's just at the end of the street, Dad.'

'Good,' he said. 'Come on, then, my dear. We'll get Grandma to come with us, eh?'

She watched them go out, then closed the door before she went and stood behind Peter. Her hand moved out tentatively and touched his sleeve. She said softly, 'Peter.'

When he pulled his arm sharply from her touch and gave her a long, cold stare, she found she could say nothing, not a word. She watched him throw the boots he was cleaning into the bottom of the cupboard, then abruptly leave the kitchen.

She stood biting her lip. He had looked at her as if he hated her. Oh, Peter.

The front door banged on Sheila's voice saying, 'There's three little ducks and four big ones in the pond, Granddad.' Then the house became quiet but for Peter's step in the bedroom above.

Oh, she must straighten things out, and at this very moment. She must.

She ran out of the kitchen, up the stairs, and burst into the bedroom. Hands in pockets, Peter was standing before the window, looking down into the garden. At her entrance he turned sharply and cried, 'I know all you're going to say. I know all the arguments you're going to use. I've heard them all before. My mother could write a book on them. You only need a little priming and you're all set to go. She's the best tutor in the world. But let me tell you something right away. You're not going to make me like she's made Dad.'

He stopped abruptly and his face twisted. Then he went on, his voice dropping to a whisper now, 'I was so sure of you.' His head was bent and he lowered himself down on to the window-seat.

'Oh, Peter. Peter, darling, go on being sure of me. Never stop being sure of me.' She hurled herself against him, pressing him tightly to her. 'I love you, I love cricket . . . I mean, I know you love cricket and I don't want you to give it up. Never . . . never. Neither your mother nor anyone else could make me . . .'

Slowly pressing her from him, he gazed into her face. And through the blur of her tears she saw the closed look lift from his face, and his eyes shone as he said, 'You know what you're saying, Betty? But I thought – I thought you were trying to stop me playing. All these weeks things have been strained. There was something, wasn't there?'

'Yes, darling, yes, there was. But not any more. Never any more.'

'Oh, Betty. Betty love, to hear you say that, to know that I haven't got to fight you to save myself from becoming like Dad. Oh,' he closed his eyes and his head dropped back on his shoulders, 'oh, you don't know what it means. It's like a new lease of life.' He pulled her roughly to him, pressing her head down into the crook of his shoulder, holding her so close that the pressure of his arms hurt.

And so they sat, quiet and still, with the wonder of their happiness enfolding them again. And Betty gazed in rapturous contentment down into the garden until a strange and disturbing object brought itself to her attention. So strange was this object in its implication that she found herself stiffening in Peter's arms.

From under the porch outside the kitchen door that was only large enough to hold a deck-chair protruded the toe of a shoe. It was brown and glossy and slightly pointed, and it was moving in quick impatient taps.

Good Lord! Peter's mother was sitting there. Oh dear, dear, for this to happen! She hadn't gone out, she'd been sitting there all the time listening. Oh, what had Peter said? She must get him away in case he started again.

She took his hand and half rose, whispering, 'Come downstairs, darling, and talk to me.'

'Why not here?' he asked lazily.

'I've got heaps to do, darling.'

'Nothing that can't wait, because I've got my wife back.' He pulled her down to him again and kissed her long and hard. 'Do you realise, Mrs Davenport, that I've been very worried, and that's putting it mildly? Gosh, how worried and scared I've been. But you'd understand, darling, if you knew what a life Dad's had.'

'Ssh!'

'It's all right, there's no-one in, they're both out. And it's about time I told you anyway, so you'll understand why I adopted the attitude I did about cricket.'

The toe was still tapping away, only quicker now, and suddenly Betty thought, She deserves all that's coming. Let him go on, let him say what he will.

'You know, Betty, you mightn't believe it, but I've

wanted to cry many a time at the sight of Dad's face as he watched me going off to a match. In fact, there were times when I did cry. There was a wood behind our house and I used to go there and get it over. But all through the match I'd be seeing his eyes, wistful and lost. It wasn't that he hadn't any courage. He had plenty except where she was concerned. He loved her and he wanted to make her happy and the only way to do that, apparently, was to give up his cricket. He told me just before we were married that if he'd had his cricket he would have considered that theirs was the happiest marriage on earth. He asked me if I was sure of you, for, he said, women sometimes ask a big price for the love they give you. You think it's worth it at the time but as the years go on you sometimes wonder if you haven't been overcharged.'

Out of the corner of her eye Betty saw the toe had ceased to move.

'She was a good mother but I nearly got to hate her for what she did to Dad. He would sneak off in the evening to watch the school play, and sometimes when he could he'd meet me on the quiet and talk cricket, cricket, cricket all the time. Every weekend she would have something on for him, all worked out, all cut and dried, everything timed to the limit. I've even seen her throw a bad turn a few minutes before he came in. This was when she knew he was determined to go and watch a good game, such as a county match. You wouldn't believe, Betty, how often this happened. I mean the possessiveness, the wanting to own Dad, body, soul and spirit. And the odd thing is, she lost him. She doesn't own any part of him now, for he's withdrawn into himself to some place where she can't follow. His dreams have taken the place of cricket and she can't get to them. She's defeating herself. Soon she'll have lost altogether . . . Why! My darling,' Peter suddenly exclaimed, 'don't cry like that.'

But Betty was sobbing helplessly. The foot had been withdrawn. It was cruel, cruel, she thought, to have let her listen. I should have stopped him. Oh, it was cruel of me.

She pulled herself gently away from Peter's arms as she heard steps on the stairs, and the next moment Mrs Davenport's voice came from the landing, light and airy, saying, 'I'm going to lie down for a while, Betty. I've got a bad head. I've been trying to drop off in the drawing room, but I couldn't manage it.'

Quickly, sniffing and coughing, Betty forced herself to reply equally lightly: 'All right, Mam, I'm changing, but I'll bring you something up in a little while.'

As she was talking she was looking at Peter, and he exclaimed under his breath, 'Good Lord! She must have been in all the time. Whew! It's a good job she was in the drawing room. Lord – and the things I've said.' He wiped his brow. 'If she'd heard me!' He gave a little nervous laugh. 'I've always wanted to tell her but I could never bring myself to it. It's difficult to tell your mother things like that. Oh, boy, if she'd heard . . .'

Visualising the woman in the room across the

landing, alone with only the opinion of her son for company, Betty suddenly felt an immense pity rise in her, and she had the urge to go to her mother-in-law and comfort her, for she realised now how near she had been to wanting to possess Peter, body, soul and spirit. But she had been halted in time, she had been given a second chance. And who had given her that chance? Why, Peter's mother herself.

Peter was saying, 'Darling, we'll have to fall in with her wishes for the time she's here,' and she answered, 'Yes; yes, we'll do what she wants,' and as they went quietly downstairs she wondered what her mother-in-law's wishes were at this moment . . .

By seven o'clock Mr Davenport had tripped up and downstairs three times and reported that Mam was still asleep.

Betty had gone quietly into the room too and looked down at her mother-in-law. Her face, buried half in the pillow and half by her raised arm, was giving nothing away. Her breathing was regular but her body looked stiff and taut, and Betty wondered how long she would keep it up. She would have to come downstairs sometime.

When finally Mrs Davenport did come downstairs Betty found herself silent with admiration for this woman whom she alternately disliked and pitied.

She had just given final orders to Sheila that it was bed, and no more excuses were to be taken, it was over an hour past her usual time already, when Mrs Davenport came in, talking.

'I knew what it would be when I sat facing that

engine – a splitting head. And not only that, I've caught a cold in my eyes. Have you got any lotion I could use, Betty? Hello, there, my pet, aren't you in bed yet?' She gathered Sheila into her arms.

'Good gracious, Frances,' said Mr Davenport. 'You *have* caught a cold. Your eyes are all inflamed. Dear, dear.'

'Now, don't fuss,' she said to her husband. 'They'll be all right once I've bathed them.'

'They must be painful, Mam,' said Peter. 'They look sore – you'd think you'd been . . .' He didn't finish, for he could not associate crying with his mother.

Mrs Davenport looked at her son for a moment, and Betty, catching the look, turned away, and a lump, rising to her throat, threatened her own collapse.

'Yes, son, they are a bit sore. I'll be more careful in future.'

'Come along now, Sheila, say goodnight to Grandma.'

'Just one more game. Will you play the silly mid-on game, Grandma?'

'Silly mid-on game?' repeated Mrs Davenport slowly. 'Well, not tonight, my dear, but tomorrow we'll go and see Daddy playing the silly mid-on game, eh?'

'Granddad too?'

'Granddad too.'

Peter and Mr Davenport exchanged quick glances.

'And we'll go on Sunday in the bus, Grandma,

into the country and sit on the grass and have buns with icing on?' asked Sheila.

'Yes, we'll go on Sunday in the bus and sit on the grass.'

Mr Davenport sat down slowly on a chair, and a silence came over the kitchen.

Betty was thinking, I could never have done it, she's big in spite of everything, when Sheila let out a cry, startling them all. 'Look!' she screamed, pointing to the kitchen door. 'Square-leg!'

They all looked in the direction of her stubby finger. There in the doorway stood a bedraggled cat, and dangling from its mouth a long, sleek kitten.

'Square-leg, Granddad. Square-leg, Grandma. Look!'

'Yes, Square-leg it is,' said Mrs Davenport. 'And one not out.' She looked at her husband, and then at her son, and the look was so soft that they were perplexed by it and made slightly uneasy.

Later that night, lying close together in each other's arms, Peter said, 'You know, darling, I just can't believe it, but Mam seems to have changed. When I heard her say she would come to the cricket on Sunday, why, it seemed as if a miracle had happened – it seemed as if I was hearing for the first time in my life. What do you make of it, darling?'

Betty moved her cheek against his, which was as good as answering that she didn't know what to make of it, but she was thinking that a miracle *had* happened because Mrs Davenport had heard the truth about herself for the first time.

10

Blitz

John Henry Murdoch locked the door of his bed-sitting room, gave it a shake, as was his habit, picked up his case, a rug and a pillow, and made his way down the stairs.

His room was on the third floor. He sometimes wished he had paid the extra for a room on the ground floor. It would have been worth it to slip in and out without being accosted at every turn by that damned woman, Sloan.

In his mind he never called her anything else. He wasn't a man given to swearing, or her names would have been many and varied.

On reaching the last flight he stiffened. Yes, there she was, coming up from the basement. Dear, dear, he thought for probably the thousandth time, how I dislike that woman. I'll give notice. Yes, I will: war or no war, near the tube or not. But all she said to him was, 'Well, there you are, Mr Murdoch. Off to the tube again? Well, as I've said before, you're very silly, you know you're very welcome downstairs.'

'Thank you, Mrs Sloan, but I won't trouble you.'

How often had he said that to her during these

past months? He brushed past her, trying, as he always did, not to look at her lower lip. It had a strange fascination for him: it was loose and very red and wobbled from side to side when she was speaking. It did something to his stomach, made him feel almost sick, yet he never saw her but his eyes were drawn to it.

He hurried into the street, a little man with spectacles in a dark overcoat and bowler hat, one of hundreds, at that moment in London, hurrying to take shelter. He was a timid man. He had never been anything else. No-one expected anything of him; but here he was in London in the thick of it, when he could have been in a comparatively safe area. When Messrs Tollett, Tollett and Harding had asked for clerks to volunteer to remain in London as a skeleton staff to carry on a small but essential part of the business after the evacuation of the main part to safer surroundings, he had surprised himself and the departmental manager when he volunteered – or, rather, insisted in his quiet way – that he should stay behind: he had, he argued, no-one depending on him.

Mr Harris had seemed surprised – he had never troubled about Murdoch. The man worked well but had no push, no initiative. He became increasingly surprised during the following months when, without a word of comment or complaint, Murdoch had stayed behind every evening doing work others had jibbed at. Mr Harris began to notice Murdoch.

Murdoch hurried along. His thoughts were

generally ordered but that woman always had the effect of making him jumpy. He was a coward, he told himself. No, it was just that he didn't get on with women: he was afraid of them. He couldn't remember when he hadn't been. He supposed it was his many landladies who had brought this about – he had passed from one to another since his mother died. He had been seventeen then; now he was forty-two.

London's different, he reflected. This was a terrible war, but people were nicer now. Down in that tube, for the first night or two, it had been a ghastly business, but now, he had to admit, he rather liked it, much more so since he had taken up his old hobby of sketching – there were so many subjects down there. At first, the comments on his work had bothered him; they were generally gratifying but unmerited. The people in his corner were nice to him, and now they knew he did not want to talk much they left him alone.

The station entrance was thick with people, some with blankets and pillows, others with baskets or cases.

Above the noise he heard the cry of a baby, a thin wail. Sadly, he shook his head. That was truly awful.

As he entered the tunnel, he was met by a strong current of air. It whirled the ends of his rug into his face. He lifted his arm to put it down and felt his evening paper fall. The crowd jostled him on. He was vexed at losing it.

The noise on the platform was terrific. It was the

worst possible time of the evening: everyone was settling in, pegging out a claim, so to speak. A tired-looking man with an official band around his arm tried to separate the intended sleepers from the travellers.

He was shouting lustily: ''Ere, you, young 'un, stop that pushing there! Yes, sir, take the next train in, change at the Bank . . . No, missis, yer carn't put yer bed down there . . . Just because yer carn't, missis . . . Well, if yer carn't see why, leave me yer name and address, and I'll take a couple of hours off tomorrow and come and explain it all to yer.' He pushed her gently on and pointed to a space where she might find rest. 'Lummy!' he said. 'They're like kids. And you, missis, what do you say? Do I know what time the bombs will be dropped tonight? Why, of course I do! They always phone me, straight from headquarters: "Charlie," Winston says, "they're nearly 'ere." Missis, carn't yer see yer 'olding up the line? Evening, sir!' he said to Murdoch. 'The nipper's got yer bed down.'

'Thank you,' said Murdoch. 'There are more than ever tonight, don't you think?' He often had a word with this man: he admired him. He would sit for hours listening to him marshalling the people, never losing his temper, cheering the sad ones, making them laugh, often against their will. His young boy saw to Murdoch's mattress, taking it up in the morning, storing it in their house near the station, then bringing it down in the early evening ready for the night. The little fellow made quite a business of it, but Murdoch thought he earned the half-crown a week he gave him.

He reached his corner and straight away noticed that most of the usual sleepers were already there, with the odd one or two new ones.

There was a light touch on his arm. Turning, he recognised a woman he had noticed before. Her bed was near the wall at the foot of the staircase, and from this position she had a clear view of the length of the platform. He had often seen her sitting up long after the others had gone to sleep, sometimes reading, sometimes just looking about her. She was holding out his paper. 'I caught it as it fell; I was just behind you; but you were pushed on and I was unable to give it to you.'

He smiled at her shyly and thanked her; then she turned and picked her way to her bed. He was greatly embarrassed when he found he was gazing after her. But how thin she was, he thought. Her neck was scraggy. Perhaps she didn't have enough to eat. She had a nice voice, though. He found himself wondering who she was. She was always alone and, apart from a word here and there, spoke little.

After settling himself on his mattress, he started to arrange his sketching materials, while looking around for a subject, someone he could finish tonight, for they didn't always return. At the foot of his own mattress a man was lying lengthwise on the bare stone of the platform. He was looking a little fuddled, an impression accentuated by a bottle sticking out of a pocket of his jacket. His supply had evidently not run out.

On his other side, he noticed a young man he hadn't seen before. He was wearing a mackintosh and his hair was in great disorder as if he were in the habit of running his hands through it. However, it was really his face that drew Murdoch's attention: it was blank, with the blankness of despair. He was sitting with his back against the wall, his knees drawn up, his hands hanging loosely between them. His eyes were fixed on the platform, and Murdoch wondered what he was seeing there. Some tragedy, no doubt.

A commotion on his left drew his attention. The befuddled man was sitting up, helping himself to his bottle, and the occupant of the mattress nearest to him was objecting in her loudest manner: 'Look 'ere, you! I've told yer before, if yer want to guzzle, go somewhere else. I've got kids 'ere, I 'ave, and they don't see none of that at 'ome, they don't, an' what's more they ain't goin' to see any of it 'ere, if I can 'elp it. The smell of you's enough to knock down the devil, so it is. If only me man was 'ere he'd push you on that line.' At this point a guffaw from someone made her sweep a threatening glance around, which was met and returned on all sides by sober looks.

The man had returned the bottle to his pocket and he looked at her through heavy eyes as he muttered, 'To the line. Yes, that would be the best way.' Then he lay down again and made as if to sleep, which brought the added response from the woman, 'I'll call the warden, so I will,' and the chorus, 'Oh, leave the fellow alone. He's quiet enough.'

A neat little woman immediately next to Murdoch, who had been laying out a meal on two cases, said, 'Don't bother with him, Mrs Lewis. Yer never know what's made him get drunk. Sit down and have a cup of tea. Things like that isn't worth getting worked up about. Come on, now. Once he's sobered up he'll no doubt move.'

The big woman allowed herself to be pacified, but kept glancing contemptuously at the hulk now lying on the foot of her mattress.

'Will you have a cup of tea, Mr Murdoch? I've got plenty,' said the little woman.

'It's very kind of you, but won't you need it before the night's out?' he answered.

'We'll have some more in a little while. My girl calls in home and makes some fresh on her way from work. You there, Georgie! Pass that to the gentleman. Mind you don't spill it, now.'

Georgie did as he was bade, and whispered, 'If me ma lets me sit up, and I don't fidget, can I watch you draw?'

Murdoch did not like anyone watching him sketch, it made him nervous, but with the tea in his hand and remembering other kindnesses from his neighbour, he said, 'Yes, of course.'

But his tea took decidedly the wrong channel when he heard Georgie say, 'Can I sit up for a while, Mum? Mr Murdoch says he would like me to sit and watch him sketching: I might learn something.'

'All right, but only for a little while,' said his mother. 'And, mind, don't trouble the gentleman.'

Murdoch and Georgie looked at each other. Murdoch had to smile.

The couple to his right had just come in. Generally, they seemed very jolly and, Murdoch thought, very much in love, too. He judged that they hadn't been long married. Tonight, however, they were quiet: the girl's face was red and swollen, the man's sad, bewildered.

Murdoch ventured quietly, 'I hope there's nothing wrong.'

The young man sat down heavily. 'We copped it last night,' he said. 'Every stick gone, not a damn thing left – after waiting five years, and both working our guts out to get the place together. Everything was paid for; that's how we wanted it; and now it's gone.'

The girl began to sob, and he gathered her into his arms.

'You still have each other; that's everything,' said Murdoch.

'Yes,' said the young man, 'but it's damned hard.' He drew a rug over the sobbing girl, and they lay down together.

It's damned hard. The words echoed in his mind.

He looked along the crowded platform, at the hundreds of figures lying or sitting there. For all of them it was damned hard; for a few it was terrible. As if to include her in this group he turned to look towards the thin woman, as he now mentally called her. Why should it be worse for her than for the others? he questioned himself. Perhaps because, like himself, she was alone.

'Are you going to draw the skinny woman, Mr Murdoch?' said Georgie, trying to be helpful.

Murdoch rounded on the unfortunate Georgie, surprising himself at the heat in his voice: 'Please do not use that term when you talk of the lady! You are very rude.'

A little bewildered, Georgie muttered, 'I ain't said nothing. You was looking at her, so I thought you was going to draw her.'

Yes, thought Murdoch, he's quite right. Silly of me. Aloud, he said, 'Yes, I see; but skinny isn't a very nice word, and I'm sure it would hurt her to hear it.'

'But 'ow could she 'ear it in this noise?' Georgie screamed, to make himself heard above the noise of an incoming train. 'An' I wasn't callin' her names.'

The train had stopped before Georgie finished; and his mother demanded, ''Ave yer gone mad, yellin' like that? 'Ere, sit down.' And she caught him by the seat of his pants, and he met the mattress none too gently.

This last question was too much for Georgie: tears welled in his eyes; his lip trembled; he looked reproachfully at Murdoch, who was extremely nervous that Georgie might start to cry and perhaps wail out the whole matter to his mother, when the word skinny might even reach the ears of the lady herself. He made reparation in the only way he could: 'It's my fault, Mrs Pollock,' he said. 'I was explaining to Georgie, when the train came in, to sit down at the foot of my mattress in a certain position so that I could sketch him.' And turning back to Georgie, he said, 'Now, if you'll just sit there, Georgie, and look down towards the end of the platform.'

Mollified, Georgie tumbled into the desired position, his tears replaced with a grin.

'It's very good of you indeed,' said his mother. 'Oh, Georgie, if it comes out all right, we'll send it to your pop.'

Georgie sat with a fixed expression, his lips tight, his eyes wide, all his muscles tense, and no amount of persuasion on Murdoch's part could make him relax: he was 'bein' drew', and he knew how to sit when he was 'bein' drew'.

After a time, Murdoch gave it up and proceeded to draw a likeness as unlike Georgie at the present time as possible.

An hour passed. Georgie's sister had arrived, and with her a plentiful supply of hot tea, and Georgie had been persuaded to relax and to have his supper; the young couple were asleep. The big woman, Murdoch noticed, had been joined by her husband, who didn't look the kind of man who would push anyone on to a line without a good cause: he was as good-tempered as his wife was bad, Murdoch considered. It was evident he wasn't going to be persuaded to carry out his wife's wishes. 'Who the hell's he disturbing, Maggie?' was his answer. 'You won't find me movin' in on 'im. Not if I could. Now shut yer blankety mouth, Maggie, an' let's have a bit of supper. What d'you say, Mrs Pollock?'

And straight away Georgie's mother agreed with him. 'But,' she added, 'I'm not 'appy in me mind about him lying like that. Another roll or two the wrong way, and 'e'd be on the line. Look, what about wakin' 'im up and givin' 'im a strong cup of tea? It might pull 'im together.' And she looked around her and asked Murdoch what he thought. He said it would be the wisest thing to do.

'Will you waken him, Mr Lewis?' she said.

'Yes, I'll stir him,' he said. 'But mind you keep yer mouth shut, Maggie.'

Kneeling on the mattress by the sleeping man, he shook him gently, the while saying, 'I say, mate, c'mon, show a leg!' Another shake brought a stirring. The man opened his eyes and lay gazing at the large, kindly face looking down at him.

He was evidently much sobered. 'Who are you?' he said. 'Where am I?' The well-modulated voice was in contrast to his dirty unshaven appearance.

'Why, mate, you're in the tube. C'mon! Sit up an' 'ave a swill of tea. Then yer'll see where yer are, all right.' And he helped the man to a sitting position at the foot of the mattress.

Apparently bewildered, the man gazed about him. His hand went to his head: 'How did I get here?' he said.

'Search me,' said Mr Lewis. 'Me wife was the first down 'ere of this little gang, and you were already 'ere, dead to the world.'

'Was I alone?' he asked; then, 'Where's Marjory? What's the date?'

'Search me again. What's the bloomin' date? Oh,

wait a minute! That gent'll know. What's the date, sir?' he asked Murdoch.

'Friday the twenty-fourth of January,' Murdoch answered.

''Ere! Drink this cup of tea,' said Mrs Pollock; 'it'll clear yer 'ead, then p'raps you'll remember.'

The man took the tea, but did not drink it: he looked from one to another of them, his brows knit tightly together. Then, 'It happened on Sunday,' he said. 'Where've I been since then?' His eyes were appealing to Lewis. 'Where's Marjory? She didn't come down here with me, did she?'

'Look here, mate: tell us what's happened. We'll help you if we can. Drink this tea; yer'll feel better. No, yer came down 'ere alone, as far as I can gather.'

'But what've I been doing since Sunday?' he muttered. 'It was when I got home with Marjory. The house was down, and she was in it – my wife was in it, under it. We worked for hours.' He looked down at his hands: they were swollen and torn; the skin was off in many places. 'And then,' he said, 'they dropped incendiaries, dozens of them. There was nothing left, nothing. I ran. I kept running: I don't know where I've been. But I must find Marjory. She's my little girl.' He staggered to his feet and would have fallen, had not Lewis steadied him. 'Thank you. I'm sorry I'm in this state, but it was terrible. Thank you again for your kindness,' and with this he nodded to Mrs Pollock and stumbled along the platform.

'Here, Maggie, give me me coat,' said Lewis.

'And where d'yer think you're going?' wailed Maggie.

'I'm goin' with that bloke to find his kid. That's where I'm goin'. Can't yer see it's not drink that's the matter with him? Now, for God's sake, shut up! Yes, I know there's a blitz on. Now, Maggie,' he patted her on the shoulder, 'be your age. See yer soon.' And he was off down the platform.

Murdoch saw him reach the stumbling figure and take his arm, before they disappeared into the milling crowd.

Mrs Lewis started to cry noisily. 'He'll be blown to bits, so he will; listen to them bombs! He'll never get back. Oh dear! What will I do if I'm left a widda? Oh! What'll become of me?'

'Don't be so soft. Yer don't 'ear any bombs down 'ere,' said Mrs Pollock, 'so shut up now. He'll come back large as life, you'll see. If yer wake up that young couple with your noise I'll give yer a push, so 'elp me. Look, lie down and I'll cover you up. I think we'll all turn in; it's nearly ten anyway. Come on, Georgie; Mr Murdoch'll finish yer tomorrer, won't you, Mr Murdoch?'

With many grumbles Georgie took off his boots and coat and snuggled under the rug at the bottom end of the mattress, the while kicking his sister, lying at the top end, which brought an appeal from her to her mother.

Georgie's ears were boxed, but apart from a few snuffles, peace reigned. Those who weren't already settled down now prepared to do so.

Apart from the occasional noise of trains, the station was quiet.

Murdoch sat with his back pressed against the wall, trying to read. But he could not settle to his book: he kept thinking of Lewis and the man. He was glad the man hadn't been allowed to go alone. He would have liked to go, too, but his shyness had prevented him offering.

His eyes strayed, as they often had already that evening, to the thin woman. She was writing in a notebook.

She's plain, he thought, but with that plainness that needs just a touch to make it beautiful.

She looked up, caught his glance and smiled. He smiled back, but became flustered with his daring. He put his book back into his case, arranged his pillow and lay down.

Mrs Pollock, too, lay down, alongside her daughter. 'God help them up above,' she said. It was her goodnight prayer. She was soon asleep.

As Murdoch lay awake, feeling a little sad and more lonely than ever tonight, he wondered when it would all cease. He would not welcome normal life again: it had been too quiet, too fruitless. Although naturally a quiet man he had become almost a recluse: he did not long for the company of his fellow creatures in herds, as he had it on these nights, but for that of one or two individuals whom he might call 'friends' – not friends like Smithson at the office, who frequently invited him at weekends to soak in the pleasures afforded by some badly tarnished female, but for someone with whom he could talk; yes, and for someone with whom he could sit before a friendly fire and not talk.

He looked at his watch. It was nearly eleven. Time he was asleep, he reflected.

He must have dozed, for he was aroused by sleepy voices enquiring none too politely what the blankety row was about.

He roused himself and, leaning on an elbow, looked towards the middle entrance to the platform from where the noise was coming. The sight that met his eyes woke him completely. He sat up and hurriedly put on his spectacles to make sure he was seeing aright. On all sides of him, it seemed that people were rousing themselves and complaining, but above them rose the voice of the tube warden who, earlier, had good-temperedly marshalled the people to their places. It was evident that his patience was wearing thin and would soon join that of a porter near him, who, from the sound of it, had lost his.

'Look 'ere, lady, see that train that's just gone out? That's the last one goes to King's Cross, and even if yer 'ad taken it, yer would 'ave been bundled in just the same kind of station yer in now, an' kept there for the night.'

'I would have you understand I am not staying in any station for any part of the night. I am taking a train from King's Cross north at midnight. Will you be good enough to show me out of this smelly rabbit warren?'

Murdoch realised he was muttering, 'She looks magnificent. She sounds magnificent. I wonder who she is. What wonderful white hair! I've never seen anything like it. I doubt if anyone here has ever seen anyone like her. What a bearing. And the boy with her . . .'

Mrs Pollock broke in on his thoughts. 'What's the likes of 'er want down 'ere? I should think that fur cloak she's wearing could buy 'er a station all to 'erself. You lie down there, Georgie! There's nothin' fer you to see. I say, Mr Murdoch, they're comin' this way. Yes, she does look grand, don't she? She must be well over sixty and still as straight as a die. Will you lie down there, Georgie!' And Georgie was thrust back.

Led by the imperious old lady, with a boy of about thirteen, the porter and the warden close on her heels, the cavalcade passed by, the warden answering whispered enquiries with facial contortions and eloquent jerks of his thumb.

The procession stopped abruptly. The old lady was staring at a girl, evidently a late-comer, who was unconcernedly putting her blonde hair in curlers. On a case in front of her was a bottle of setting lotion and a jar of cream. Her face was already creamed for the night.

The haughty stare in no way intimidated the girl: she merely returned it with raised eyebrows. The old lady snapped her gaze to the luckless porter.

'If my car is not in order,' she said, 'will you kindly get me a taxi? I shall go to the nearest hotel.'

The porter spread out his hands in appeal as he replied, 'Lady, your car is not in working order, your chauffeur is receiving first aid, and if you could get a taxi it wouldn't get through that blitz without something happening. You shouldn't have to be reminded, madam, that there's a bad raid on. It really is a wonder you're alive, with the lump of stuff that hit your car. Now, if you'll only be patient and stay down here for a few hours. Anyway,' he finished with finality, 'you'll just have to make the best of it, and it isn't such a bad best at present, as you'll find out if those fires up above get nearer.' And with this, he turned away saying, 'I'm going. I've wasted enough time. And what thanks do you get?'

'But this is outrageous! You just can't leave me down here. You!' She turned to the warden. 'Stop that porter.' But he ignored her and turned to the boy who, until now, had seemed to treat the whole affair as a matter of course. Placing his hands kindly on the boy's shoulders, he said to him, 'Sonny, you seem a sensible lad. Now, can't you get your granny – she is your granny, isn't she? – to see reason and sit down here until the All Clear goes? Then off you can go to wherever it was you were going.'

The boy looked at him steadily for a moment before he acknowledged, 'Yes, you're right, but you know, it is pretty awful for the Gran. I don't mind. In fact, I've enjoyed the whole affair – wouldn't have missed it for anything – but, you see, the Gran—' He turned to his grandmother: 'Gran, what do you say? I suppose we could sit down here for a few hours. It's pretty hot upstairs, you know.'

'Antony, have you, too, completely lost your senses and your eyesight? Would you mind telling me where we could possibly sit in this?' She waved her hand towards the end of the platform.

'Yes, it does look pretty hopeless. But perhaps this – er – gentleman could find us some space.'

The warden looked around rather hopelessly. It seemed that even his practised eye could detect no unoccupied pitch.

Then his searching glance alighted on Mr Murdoch sitting alone on his mattress in comparative luxury compared with the situation of his companions.

'Just a tick, young man. I think I might be able to fix you up.' Now, the momentary cynosure of all eyes, he hurried down to Murdoch.

'I say, sir,' he said. 'I know it's a lot to ask, but you see how we're fixed. Would you let them sit down here beside you? It'll only be for a little while; and to tell you the truth, sir, the old battle-axe has got me a little worn out. You wouldn't believe it, sir, the talking we've had to do to get her *down* here. The youngster's all right, a pretty cool customer for a young 'un, if you ask me. Now what d'you say?'

Murdoch was evidently much agitated by the request: 'I see your problem,' he stammered. 'Well, they are very welcome to sit here, but the old lady is rather . . . well, is rather . . . well, you see what I mean, I'm afraid it will be very unpleasant for her. But of course, if you can't find any other place . . . they will have to sit somewhere,' he finished.

'Thank you, sir. I tell you plainly, I'll be damned glad to get them settled. It's the first time I've had to deal with anyone like her, and I hope it's the last.'

He beckoned to the boy, who came to him at once. 'Look here, sonny. This gentleman will let you sit with him. Now, do you think you could persuade your granny to come along?'

'Yes, I think I'll be able to manage that,' the boy answered brightly. Then, turning to Murdoch, he said, 'Thank you, sir. It's very kind of you to do this. My grandmother is rather tired, and when she's tired . . . well, you understand, sir, don't you? I'll go and bring her.'

'That's a nice kid. He's certainly all right, isn't he?'

'Yes, exceptionally nice,' said Murdoch. 'Apparently he doesn't take after his grandmother.'

'You're right there,' put in Mrs Pollock. 'You're not goin' to 'ave any too comfortable a night, Mr Murdoch. But better you than me. I'm afraid I'd lose me temper. Georgie! Will you lie down there, before I skelp yer. An' don't gape like that! Shut yer mouth, yer not at the zoo. Get off to sleep this minute!'

But sleep was far from Georgie: he watched the boy approaching, followed by the old lady. His ears were as open as his mouth; he was taking in every word.

'This is the gentleman, Gran.'

Murdoch, who had hurriedly put on his jacket and straightened the rug, was standing up. He felt smaller than ever against this tall, thin, cold figure.

'You are very welcome, madam,' he said. 'It is poor comfort, but I am afraid it is the best there is to offer you.' His voice was trailing away into nothing. Words were difficult for him at all times, but the stare from those steely eyes froze him.

It was the boy who again came to the rescue. 'Sit down here, Gran,' he said. 'You must be pretty tired. Perhaps you'll get a little sleep.'

'Sleep?' She looked at her grandson in astonishment. 'In this? However, I'll have something to say about all this tomorrow.' She returned a last cold stare to the many eyes still on her, then sat down on the mattress with the ease of a young girl.

The boy sat beside her; but Murdoch, now more uncomfortable perhaps than at any other time in his life, remained standing for some seconds, uncertain of what he should do. Were he to sit down he would have to rub shoulders with that austere figure; he just couldn't pluck up courage to do so.

Slowly, she turned her head and looked at him. 'Do you intend to stand like that all night?' she demanded. 'Stop fidgeting and sit down.'

It was a command given by one who wasn't in the habit of repeating herself. What Murdoch would have done he never knew for the young man next to him, awakened like the rest, tapped his leg and said, 'A woman over there is trying to catch your eye.'

He looked, and the thin woman was beckoning to him. He glanced round to make sure it was him she meant. He was feeling rather flustered. He excused himself, and picked his way towards her.

It was like coming from the frozen north into warm sunshine, he thought.

'I can see you're in difficulties,' the woman greeted him. 'Would it help matters if we changed places? You'd at least be able to sit down here. I have no mattress but these rugs aren't too bad.'

He did not know how to thank her. 'It is more than kind of you,' he said. 'I must confess to being overpowered by the old lady. I couldn't imagine just how I was going to spend the night. Are you sure you don't mind doing this? You're going to find it very unpleasant.'

She stood up. 'Don't worry,' she said, smiling. 'We'll get along all right. She can't be so bad to have a grandson like that. I'll leave my case here; I can get it in the morning. Goodnight. Try to get some sleep.' And she was gone, leaving him with a sense of warmth.

She was so nice: she put one at one's ease. He did not feel afraid of her.

He lay down. It was very hard, but he was happy to be there.

When she reached Murdoch's place she was met with a glare from the old lady. Nothing daunted, she sat down.

'I'm Mary Stafford,' she said. 'I thought this would be a better arrangement. Perhaps we could lie down.'

But she was cut short: 'I have no intention of lying down. Please don't include me in your arrangements.'

'Just as you please,' Mary answered. 'But your grandson looks rather tired; I'm sure he would find sitting up all night rather a strain.'

'You're right, miss,' broke in Mrs Pollock. 'If some folks want to sit up all night, they needn't take it out on the kids. Look 'ere, Mrs Lewis, would you let my Lucy sleep with you till your man comes, so the young gent can sleep with Georgie? That's if you will, sonny,' she said to Antony.

The young boy looked at his grandmother. 'I would like to, Gran,' he said. 'It will give you more room.'

What protest she might have made was silenced when she noticed the signs of fatigue on the boy's face. 'As you please,' she snapped. 'Nothing is impossible on a night like this. The world is mad. Everybody's mad.'

She looked at the boy with whom it was being proposed her grandson should sleep. Her nose wrinkled in distaste, and her lips were more tightly pressed together. She looked along the railway line and continued to do so. With no support to her back she sat bolt upright and remained so far into the night.

The regular sleepers lost interest; there was nothing more to see. They lay down and slept. But not so Georgie and his companion when, with further motherly concern, Mrs Pollock tucked them in. They lay so close that Georgie was disconcerted. He blinked, wriggled a little, scratched his nose and opened his mouth to speak, but no sound came. He closed it again and continued to blink.

Antony, too, was not feeling any too comfortable. It must be pretty ghastly if one had to lie like this every night. He was no longer feeling sleepy, he felt curious.

'Do you sleep here every night?' he whispered.

Georgie stopped blinking and nodded.

'Why? Has your house been bombed?'

'Twice,' Georgie whispered hoarsely, holding up two fingers to make himself doubly clear.

'I say! That's awful. Can't you get away from London?'

'Don't want to,' said Georgie. 'Rather stay with me mum.'

They were silent again. Georgie had stopped blinking; he was feeling more himself again. 'Where yer from?' he whispered.

'Well, I'm from Sussex. That's where my father lives. But I spend most vacs with Gran.'

'Where does she live?' said Georgie.

'Oh, in Cumberland. She has a place in London, but she doesn't like London, so that's shut up.'

'Two houses!' Georgie's eyes were wide. 'Are they big 'uns?'

'Fairly,' said Antony. 'But that doesn't matter. I like small houses best . . . and dogs, we have grand dogs.'

'I bet you haven't any horses.'

'Well, as a matter of fact we have quite a decent stable.'

'Oh . . . well. I bet you didn't mean what you said about liking small houses.'

'Yes, I did. I should like to live in a house with only three rooms, and a bath, of course. So would

Gran. But, of course, she's got to live in a big house and see to the estate. She doesn't like living like that. And it's this that makes her cross and frighten the whole family.'

'She's an awful old dame,' said Georgie. 'Crikey! Aren't I glad she's not me mum! How big is her family?' He could never get the idea of a thing unless he knew the size of it.

'Oh, gosh! I just can't tell you how many there are offhand. There are uncles and aunts and great-aunts and cousins but, of course, they don't all live with us; they just come and visit.'

'And does she frighten the lot of them?' asked Georgie. 'And aren't you frightened of her?'

'Oh, no, we're pals. But she does lay it on thick with the others.' He laughed quietly. 'You see, she's very rich.'

'She's an awful old dame,' Georgie repeated; then he asked, 'Where'd yer go to school?'

'Well, at present I'm at Eton, but I've been ill and I'm not going back for a week or two.'

'I'm leavin' next year,' vouchsafed Georgie. 'When d'yer leave?'

'Oh, not for some time yet; then I'll be going to Oxford.'

'We went on a trip to Southend two years ago,' said Georgie, completely himself now and not to be outdone.

It was entirely in Antony's favour that he passed this over without even a smile.

'Does your father work in London?' he asked.

'No, he's in the army – Pay Corps. He's a corporal,' George answered proudly. 'He's got two stripes on there.' He pointed to his arm under the blanket.

There was a violent wriggle at the top of the mattress and a hand caught Antony fairly on the buttocks and a muffled voice said, 'Now, Georgie, will yer stop that talkin' an' go to sleep?'

The colour must have flooded Antony's face. This was the first time in his memory that he had had his bottom smacked.

Georgie clapped his two hands over his mouth to stifle the sound of his laughter.

Then Antony began to laugh, spasmodically at first, until he, too, had to sink his head into the mattress to deaden the sound.

'She thought you was me,' gasped Georgie. And they continued their conversation, but in a low whisper.

John Murdoch woke later than usual next morning. It was six thirty. Hearing a voice like muffled thunder, he roused himself. All about him were pale, drawn faces and stuffy eyes. Only here and there shone out the bright countenance of some un-daunted spirit. It was always like this first thing. After a cup of tea they would feel differently.

He reflected he could do with a cup himself. He was cold and cramped.

As he folded the blankets he wondered how she managed them: they were quite a weight. Then a voice behind him said, 'How did you sleep?'

He turned quickly, and there she stood with his case, pillow and rug in her arms.

'Oh!' he said. 'Good morning. I slept quite well. Yes, quite well, thank you. And you? Have our guests gone?' he asked, looking past her to the place where he usually slept. 'You know, I had quite forgotten about them. How I could dare to forget about that old lady, I don't know.' They both laughed.

'They left more than an hour ago,' she answered. 'I don't think she slept at all, even for a short time. I woke three times and she was still sitting up wide-eyed each time. However, something funny happened. Early on Mrs Pollock smacked the boy in mistake for Georgie. I happened to be awake and I could hear them both laughing. They seemed to be on very friendly terms. In fact, Georgie now seems quite crestfallen that they are gone.'

'Yes,' Murdoch said, 'he was a nice boy; but his grandmother,' he shook his head, 'I'm afraid she frightened me more than any raid would have the power to do . . . By the way, what do you do with your blankets?'

'Oh, I leave them at the canteen,' she answered.

'Then you must let me help you. If you'll carry my case with your own, I'll manage the rest of the things. Oh, yes!' he insisted. 'I will carry them. They're really much too heavy for you.'

She made no further protest, and together – he with the appearance of a pack mule – they climbed the escalator into the cold, dark entrance. He talked quite freely with an ease that surprised himself. She told him she was a voluntary worker at the canteen near the station, giving her mornings entirely to the work. During the rest of the day she wrote things – things that were rarely published, she added, laughing.

Outside, he insisted he would carry her bags to the canteen, which was but a ten-minute walk away. Here and there they remarked on buildings now demolished that they remembered standing yesterday.

'It's dreadful,' she said. 'More people homeless. At one time it used to make me feel quite ill but, like everyone else, now I'm getting used to it. And I'm thankful for the tube, even if we are packed like herrings.'

'Yes,' he answered, 'it has been a godsend, the means of saving what must be thousands of lives. However, I'm afraid, after next week I'll not be seeing so much of them. Now that I've caught up with the backlog I don't have to work late at the office, and I'm able to join the Auxiliary Fire Service. I feel I should do something.'

'Yes,' she said, 'I know that feeling: I, too, have felt that way. My days used to be all my own; then, at the beginning of the war, I felt shy of offering my services – I couldn't see what I could do. Then one day the landlady of the rooms where I stay asked me if I would care to go with her to the canteen that afternoon and help. That was eleven months ago. I haven't missed a day since, and I love it . . . Here we are,' she added, stopping outside a large empty shop window. 'Thank you so much for carrying my things.'

'It has been a pleasure,' he answered her truthfully, 'and so little in return for your kindness of last night. I'll see you tonight, then?'

'Yes. Yes, we'll meet tonight.'

Murdoch did not look so short as he walked away. On his face was an unfamiliar expression. He had something to look forward to. Oh, yes; not only something but someone.

And she liked him. He knew she did. He sensed somehow she was a pattern of himself: small, plain, and lonely for love. Yes, that was it, lonely for love.

ROSIE OF THE RIVER
by Catherine Cookson

Sally Carpenter can't swim and doesn't like boats, so when her husband Fred announces that he has booked them a boating holiday on the Norfolk Broads she's far from enthusiastic.

Together with their beloved bull-terrier Bill they set off, only to lurch from one mishap to another. Drowning their sorrows in a local pub one evening they meet Rosie, whose family is also boating on the broads. The Carpenters befriend fifteen-year-old Rosie and when she has a fight with her violent mother it is to Fred and Sally that she runs.

After the holiday, Rosie goes to live with her grand-mother, but through the years that follow she relies on Fred and Sally whenever she is in trouble. They help her sort out the many and varied difficulties facing her in her new life, and come to look upon her as the daughter they never had.

0 552 14712 5

A SELECTION OF OTHER CATHERINE COOKSON TITLES AVAILABLE FROM CORGI BOOKS

THE PRICES SHOWN BELOW WERE CORRECT AT THE TIME OF GOING TO PRESS. HOWEVER TRANSWORLD PUBLISHERS RESERVE THE RIGHT TO SHOW NEW RETAIL PRICES ON COVERS WHICH MAY DIFFER FROM THOSE PREVIOUSLY ADVERTISED IN THE TEXT OR ELSEWHERE.

14624 2	BILL BAILEY OMNIBUS	£7.99
14609 9	THE BLIND YEARS	£5.99
14533 5	THE BONDAGE OF LOVE	£5.99
14531 9	THE BONNY DAWN	£5.99
14348 0	THE BRANDED MAN	£6.99
14156 9	THE DESERT CROP	£5.99
14705 2	THE GARMENT & SLINKY JANE	£6.99
13685 9	THE GOLDEN STRAW	£6.99
14703 6	THE HAMILTON TRILOGY	£6.99
14704 4	HANNAH MASSEY & THE FIFTEEN STREETS	£5.99
13300 0	THE HARROGATE SECRET	£5.99
14701 X	HERITAGE OF FOLLY & THE FEN TIGER	£6.99
14610 2	A HOUSE DIVIDED	£5.99
13303 5	THE HOUSE OF WOMEN	£5.99
14700 1	THE IRON FAÇADE & HOUSE OF MEN	£5.99
13622 0	JUSTICE IS A WOMAN	£5.99
14702 8	KATE HANNIGAN & THE LONG CORRIDOR	£5.99
14581 5	KATE HANNIGAN'S GIRL	£5.99
14569 6	THE LADY ON MY LEFT	£5.99
14699 4	THE MALLEN TRILOGY	£7.99
13684 0	THE MALTESE ANGEL	£5.99
14157 7	THE OBSESSION	£5.99
14073 2	PURE AS THE LILY	£5.99
14155 0	RILEY	£5.99
14706 0	ROONEY & THE NICE BLOKE	£5.99
14712 5	ROSIE OF THE RIVER	£5.99
14039 2	A RUTHLESS NEED	£5.99
10541 4	THE SLOW AWAKENING	£5.99
14583 1	THE SOLACE OF SIN	£5.99
14683 8	TILLY TROTTER OMNIBUS	£6.99
14038 4	THE TINKER'S GIRL	£5.99
14037 6	THE UPSTART	£5.99
12368 4	THE WHIP	£5.99
13577 1	THE WINGLESS BIRD	£5.99
13247 0	THE YEAR OF THE VIRGINS	£5.99

All Transworld titles are available by post from:

Bookpost, PO Box 29, Douglas, Isle of Man, IM99 1BQ

Credit cards accepted. Please telephone 01624 836000,
fax 01624 837033, Internet http://www.bookpost.co.uk
or e-mail: bookshop@enterprise.net for details

Free postage and packing in the UK. Overseas customers:
allow £1 per book (paperbacks) and £3 per book (hardbacks)